ARCTIC &
ANTARCTIC

Arctic plant

Net for catching ptarmigan

Reindeer-skin winter coat from Siberia

Siberian shaman's staff

Antarctic explorer's compass

Siberian ivory model of reindeer drawing a sled

Rosebay
willow
herb

Snowshoe
for a pony

EYEWITNESS BOOKS

ARCTIC &
ANTARCTIC

Written by
BARBARA TAYLOR

Photographed by
GEOFF BRIGHTLING

Carving of polar
bear from Canada

ALFRED A. KNOPF • NEW YORK

Model of Greenland canoe

Engraved ivory

DK

A DORLING KINDERSLEY BOOK

Cribbage board
made from
walrus tusk

Project editor Gillian Denton
Art editor Jane Tetzlaff
Managing editor Simon Adams
Managing art editor Julia Harris
Editorial Assistance Gin Von Noorden, David Pickering
Researcher Céline Carez
Production Catherine Semark
Picture research Clive Webster

This is a Borzoi Book published by Alfred A. Knopf, Inc.

This Eyewitness ™ Book has been conceived by
Dorling Kindersley Limited and Editions Gallimard.

Manufactured in Singapore
0 9 8 7 6 5 4 3 2

Library of Congress Cataloging-in-Publication Data
Taylor, Barbara, 1954–
Arctic & Antarctic / written by Barbara Taylor; photographed
by Geoff Brightling. — 1st American ed.
p. cm. — (Eyewitness books)
"A Dorling Kindersley book" – T.p. verso.
Includes index.
1. Zoology – Polar regions – Juvenile literature. 2. Polar regions –
Juvenile literature. [1. Zoology – Polar regions. 2. Animals – Habits
and behavior. 3. Polar regions.] I. Brightling, Geoff, ill.
II. Title. III Title: Arctic and Antarctic

QL104.T48 1995
508.311—dc20
ISBN 0-679-87257-4
ISBN 0-679-97257-9 (lib. bdg.)

Filmsetting by Litho Link Ltd,
Welshpool, Powys
Color reproduction by
Colourscan, Singapore
Printed in Singapore by Toppan

Shaman's
eagle from
Siberia

Siberian shaman's apron

Both the Arctic and
Antarctic support
some plant life

Husky dogs

Contents

Snowy owl

The ends of the Earth

THE TWO POLAR REGIONS at the very ends of the Earth are among the coldest, windiest, and most remote places on the planet. A huge, frozen ocean – the Arctic – surrounds the North Pole; a vast area of frozen land – Antarctica – surrounds the South Pole. Both the Arctic and Antarctic have long, dark, freezing winters. During the short summer, the sun shines all the time, and animals flock to the polar areas to feed and nest. The Arctic and Antarctic are the last two wilderness areas on earth. However, the Arctic has already been exploited for its mineral wealth, and both polar regions are increasingly threatened by pollution, mining, and other human pressures.

The position of the Arctic and the Antarctic

TRAPPED BY THE ICE
In 1596, a Dutch explorer, William Barents, set off on his third attempt find a route from Europe to China and India around the North Pole. W his ship was trapped by sea ice, he and his crew were forced to winte ashore, building a cabin from the wrecked ship. In spring, the men set for Europe in the ship's boats. Barents himself died, but his men surviv

Long tongues of ice extend into the sea from the edges of ice sheets

An unstructured slush known as frazil ice forms below the surface

MYSTERY LAND

he 4th century B.C., the Greek philosopher Aristotle suggested the existence
f a southern landmass, known as *Terra Australis Incognita* – the unknown
uthern continent. Mapmakers included a huge southern continent on their
ps until 1773, but it was not until Captain James Cook's explorations in the
nid-18th century that anyone was able to find out what was really there.

NORTHERN LIGHTS

Auroras are wispy
curtains of light that
appear in the sky above
the poles. They can
sometimes take the
form of brilliantly
colored shooting rays.
Auroras are caused
by charged particles
from the sun striking
gases in the earth's
atmosphere above the
poles. This makes the
gases give off light.

MIDNIGHT SUN

In regions near the North
and South poles, the sun
never sets for several
months during the summer.
This happens because of the
tilt of the Earth toward the
sun. While one pole has
constant daylight, the other
is shrouded in winter
darkness because the
sun never rises.

*iet waters ice often begins as thin
s, known as grease ice because they
he water with an oily sheen*

*Freezing builds the ice into
thicker layers; wind and waves
work to break it up*

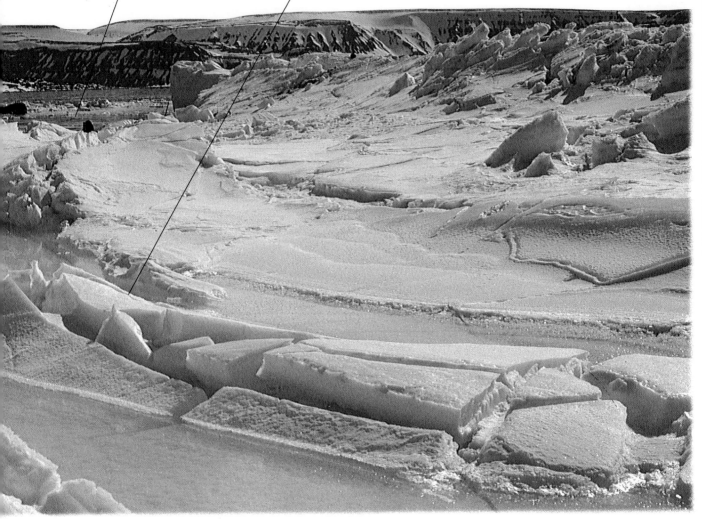

The Arctic and tundra

AT THE CENTER OF THE ARCTIC REGION is a vast area of permanently frozen ice floating on the Arctic Ocean. The Arctic region also includes the largest island in the world, Greenland, the island of Spitsbergen, and the northern edges of North America, Asia, and Europe. South of the Arctic Ocean is the tundra, which means "treeless plain" in Russian. The landscape is low and flat, with many lichens, mosses, grasses, and sprawling, low bushes. Trees cannot grow in the true Arctic because they are unable to stand up to the intense cold and fierce winter winds. Water from the warmer Pacific and Atlantic oceans sometimes flows into the Arctic Ocean, warming the sea and air and clearing ice from the coasts in summer.

MAPPING THE COAST
In 1819–1822 Sir John Franklin, who later lost his life searching for the elusive Northwest Passage (pp. 52–53), made a hazardous land expedition charting the coast of Canada. At one point he took to canoe, which was particularly dangerous as the ice was breaking up. Wooden ships and boats of the 19th century could easily be crushed or trapped by ice.

Marshy pools for because permafro prevents water f draining away

The "tree line" where forest gives way to tundra is often taken to be the southern boundary of the true Arctic

Frozen layer, called permafrost, a little way below the surface; it never thaws out

BEAR JOURNEYS
Polar bears live only in the Arctic. They make long journeys across the Arctic pack ice, hunting for seals. The bears are expert divers and swimmers, and often hitch rides on ice floes. One polar bear was found swimming 200 miles (320 km) from land. Polar bears can also dive from the top of icebergs more than 50 ft (15 m) into the water.

Icebergs that have broken off from the main ice floe

Permanent ice sheet floating on the surface of the sea

SINKING THE UNSINKABLE
Icebergs are a major hazard to ships because most of their bulk floats below the water line. The most famous iceberg casualty was the *Titanic*, supposedly unsinkable, which was sunk on her maiden voyage in April 1912. Only 705 of the 2,227 passengers and crew were rescued, because the ship did not have enough lifeboats for all the people on board.

The large area of floating ice at the edge of the main ice sheet is called pack ice

At the edges of the ocean, ice forms in winter and melts again in summer

Only low-growing plants survive on the tundra

Summer in Denali National Park, Alaska

FROZEN PROBLEMS
A permanently frozen layer called permafrost occurs a little way below the surface of the Arctic soil. It can be about 3,000 ft (900 m) thick. The land above the permafrost thaws in summer and the water collects on the surface, forming lakes and marshes. Buildings and roads have to be specially insulated to avoid melting the permafrost, or they begin to collapse. Disposal of sewage, waste water, and drainage also damages the permafrost.

Loiseleuria procumbens, *a type of grass, grows in northern Greenland*

ARCTIC PLANTS
Arctic plants have adapted in various ways to the low Arctic temperatures and a short growing season. Some can photosynthesize (make their own food) at temperatures below freezing. The plants grow rapidly in spring, taking advantage of the long periods of daylight. There are over 500 species of wildflowers, and in summer, the Arctic is ablaze with color. Some grasses have vertical leaves to catch the low-angled sunlight.

The Antarctic

THE CONTINENT OF ANTARCTICA is twice the size of Australia, and one and a half times the size of the United States. It is also three times higher than any other continent; almost all of it is covered by an ice sheet that is, on average, 8,000 ft (2,500 m) thick. This is one major reason for the extreme cold in Antarctica. The average winter temperature is -76°F (-60°C). Antarctica's harsh climate and its isolation from other continents have greatly reduced the variety of its wildlife – the largest animal that lives on land all year round is a tiny insect. During the summer, however, many animals, including penguins, whales, and seals, visit the continent to take advantage of the rich food supply and safe breeding sites around the coasts. Plants are very sparse, and consist mostly of lichens, mosses, and liverworts.

SOLE SURVIVOR
Mosses are one of the few plants able to survive in Antarctica. There are about 80 species of these tough little plants in the region. They grow in dense mats and cushions for protection from the weather. Dead moss builds up and forms banks of peat that can be several feet thick.

WARMER CLIMATE
Antarctica was not always cold. Fossil ferns (above) provide evidence of a warmer, subtropical climate about 70 million years ago. Over hundreds of millions of years, the land that is now Antarctica probably drifted to the bottom of the globe from near the equator.

SOUTH POLE PENG
Penguins live only southern hemisph the Arctic, auks ha a similar lifestyle t penguins. They als look like penguins, but auks can fly, ar penguins cannot.

Only 10 perc of an iceberg visible above water level

ICEBERGS
When snow falls on the polar plateau, it turns into ice. The ice is compacted, and flows down toward the coastal ice shelves, where it is broken up by ocean tides, currents, and waves. This is how icebergs form. Some icebergs are so large – up to 150 miles (240 km) long and 70 miles (110 km) wide – that they can be tracked by satellites for several years before they melt.

COILED CLUES
Swimming shellfish with coiled shells, called ammonites, were common in the warm seas of prehistoric times. The last ammonites died out about 65 million years ago, but fossil ammonites found on Antarctica show that Antarctic seas were warmer millions of years ago.

WEIGHT OF ICE

About 98 percent of Antarctica is covered by an immense ice sheet, which in some places is over 2.5 miles (4 km) thick. Most of the mountains, and all of the lower ground, are buried under ice. Only a few jagged peaks, called nunataks, stick out. The enormous weight of the ice pushes most of the rocky surface of Antarctica below sea level. The ice in the lowest layers of the ice sheet is thought to be at least 200,000 years old.

DRY VALLEYS

Hidden among the Transantarctic Mountains are vast dry valleys, which are bare of snow and ice for much of the year. The valleys originally dried out because the mountains held back the ice cap. Winds rushing down the valleys suck away any moisture, forming large areas of bare rock in the middle of the continent.

CLEARING THE ICE

Special ships called icebreakers are used to keep trade routes clear of ice during the winter. Before icebreakers, many early polar explorers saw their fragile wooden ships crushed by the power of the ice. Icebreakers have a specially shaped bow and a reinforced hull. They push the bow on top of the ice until the weight of the ship breaks through it.

*ergs often look blue,
ibly a reflection
the water*

Life in Antarctic waters

IN CONTRAST TO THE SMALL VARIETY of animals on the land, there is an incredible wealth of life in the sea around Antarctica. In shallow waters, ice scrapes against the seabed, preventing any life. But in deeper waters below the crust of ice, there is a greater variety of life in the Antarctic Ocean than in the Arctic Ocean. Corals and anemones are anchored to the seabed, along with some 300 varieties of sponges. Many sea creatures feed on each other or on plankton. Food is scarce for most of the year. The cold affects the life cycles of many inhabitants. Animals function more slowly. They produce fewer, larger eggs, and care for them longer. Many animals live longer than their counterparts in warmer waters. Some sponges live for several centuries.

COMMON CREATURES
Antarctic squid (top) have no shell, which may be useful in icy waters, where shells grow very slowly. They seize prey in their two long tentacles. The jellyfish (bottom), which is between 0.2 in and 20 in (0.5 and 50 cm) long, is very common in Antarctic waters.

DUAL PURPOSE SPINES
Seabed animals such as the sea urchin (*Sterechinus neumayer*) may move to shallower water during the summer, when they are not in danger from ice scouring the rocks on which they live. Their dense covering of mobile spines is used for both movement and defense.

The spines of sea urchins are often poisonous

Point at the end of the leg to dig for food in the seabed

SEA LEGS
Orange sea spiders with 10 to 12 giant legs are found in deeper Antarctic waters. The pycnogonid spider (*Decolopoda australis*) has a diameter of 6 in (15 cm). It feeds on sea anemones, and like other Antarctic sea creatures, it develops very slowly.

COLD GIANTS
Many of the Antarctic's bottom-living invertebrates (creatures without backbones) are giants, such as this giant isopod *Glyptonotus antarcticus*, a relative of the woodlouse. It fills the ecological niche occupied by crabs in other parts of the world. *Glyptonotus* grows up to 8 in (20 cm), about three times bigger than similar species elsewhere. Growth is slow in the cold waters. Slow-growing invertebrates reach larger sizes than faster-growing ones. *Glyptonotus* scavenges around the seabed and eats anything it can find.

As well as the main legs, the spider has several small ones

Tentacles of coral filter out small zooplankton drifting past

ON THE ROCKS
A rock face about 26–33 ft (8–10 m) below the surface of the water provides a good anchorage for sponges, bryozoans (sea mosses), and the long hanging stalks of the soft coral *Ascolepis*. Sponges and some corals are abundant at depths of up to 0.6 miles (1 km).

Tentacles contain stinging cells that paralyze prey

TERRIBLE TENTACLES
Sea anemones capture prey, such as small fish or starfish, in their tentacles. The tentacles then pass the prey into the central "mouth" opening, ready to be digested and absorbed into the body. Waste is also excreted through the "mouth."

R TURN
seabed around
arctica is sometimes
red with colorful red
ish. Starfish locate their prey
mell, and grasp it with rows of
feet on the underside of their
Antarctic starfish live
lives – one is
wn to have lived
e age of 39.

*feet
alking,
ng, and
ing*

Migrants and residents

THE NUMBER AND VARIETY of animals living near the poles changes dramatically with the seasons. Thousands of birds and mammals visit the Arctic or Antarctic only during the brief, light summer months, when it is warm and there is plenty of food available. In addition to the food supply, advantages for summer migrants include safe places to rear their young, few predators, and a lack of competition for food and nesting spots. Often, the same traditional migration routes are used each year, but the animals also navigate using the positions of the sun, moon, and stars, the earth's magnetic field, and familiar landmarks. Journeys are often very dangerous, and many animals are killed before reaching their destination by bad weather, lack of food, and predators. Only a few hardy animals, such as the musk ox, manage to stay in polar regions all year round.

Dense down feathers help to keep the geese warm

The [...] save en[...] by flying [...] V-formatio[...] the slipstr[...] of the [...] in [...]

Arctic tern
Sterna paradisaea

Thick skull and solid horny band protect the brain when males clash horns

Musk ox
Ovibos moschatus

Powerful wings allow the tern to cover up to 25,000 miles (40,000 km) on each round trip

CHAMPION TRAVELER
The graceful Arctic tern may see more daylight each year than any other creature. It breeds in large colonies during the Arctic summer. Then it flies all the way to the Antarctic to take advantage of the almost constant daylight and rich food supply of the Antarctic summer.

Summer feeding places
Winter breeding places
Migration route

FOOD IN THE FREEZER
Whales in both the Northern and the Southern hemispheres travel to cold polar waters in summer to take advantage of the rich food supply of plankton and fish. In winter, when the sea freezes over, they migrate back to warmer tropical waters again to breed. They eat little during their tropical stopover, relying on their immense supply of body fat, built up during the summer.

Very long outer fur retains body warmth and keeps animal dry

MIGHTY MUSK OX
Tough, hardy musk oxen roam over the harsh tundra in herds made up of females and young, led by one or more strong bulls. In summer, herds number about ten animals, but in winter, musk oxen move south, in herds of 50 or more, wherever they can find food under the snow. Their name comes from the smell given off by the males during the breeding season.

The male's antlers are larger and thicker than those of the females

Caribou
Rangifer tarandus

FLIGHT OF THE SNOW GEESE
Many thousands of pairs of snow geese nest in the Arctic tundra in the summer. They migrate all the way from the Gulf of Mexico, a journey of about 2,000 miles (3,200 km). On their journey, they fly in flocks of tens of thousands of birds. The shorter days at the end of summer tell the snow geese it is time to fly south once more.

re tucked back g flight to make a streamlined shape

Snow goose
Anser caerulescens

SUMMER HOLIDAYS
Caribou herds are always on the move, wandering between their winter and summer feeding grounds and snatching bites of food wherever they can find it. In spring, immense herds trek northward to feed on lichens and other low-growing tundra plants. They use well-marked trails that are often centuries old. As winter closes in, the caribou move south once more to the shelter of the forests.

Curved horns for defense against enemies such as wolves

Dense woolly underfur and thick layers of fat under the skin keep the musk ox warm

les are er than males

Short, very strong legs support the massive body

Edges of hooves are sharp enough to dig through thick snow or ice to reach mosses, lichens, and roots underneath

Adaptable animals

TO SURVIVE THE CONTRASTING SEASONS, animals have to change. As winter approaches, some mammals' fur coats grow thick. Winter fur is often white, which helps to camouflage the animal against snow. A thick layer of fat in their skin traps extra warmth and acts as a food store in lean times. Birds also have layers of fat and dense, fluffy feathers to keep out the cold. For many birds and mammals, the severe winter weather is just too much to cope with. They migrate south to warmer places, returning again in spring. Insects lay their eggs in the warmer soil, and the larvae are able to withstand the freezing temperatures of winter. As summer arrives, birds and mammals shed their thick coats. Animals that turn white in winter often have brown summer camouflage.

FINE FURS
People in cold countries wear fur clothes to keep warm through the coldest winters. They usually obtain them by snaring their original owners in traps.

Arctic fox
Alopex lagopus

DRESSED FOR SUMMER
In summer, the Arctic fox grows a thinner coat of brownish gray fur over most of its body. These colors match the brownish gray rocks of the tundra landscape, making the fox hard to see so that it can creep up on its prey, such as lemmings, without being spotted. The fox stores food under rocks during the summer and comes back to eat it in the winter months when food is hard to find. Arctic foxes have a varied diet – they eat anything from berries, shells, and dead animals to garbage and birds and their eggs.

The chest and belly are usually a pale grayish white

Short legs (and tail) lose less heat than long ones as there is less surface area exposed to the air

Thick, bushy tail can be curled around the body for warmth during blizzards or when resting or sleeping

Antarctic ice fish
Chaenocephalus aceratus

ANTIFREEZE IN ITS VEINS
Many Antarctic fishes have "antifreeze" molecules in their bodies that enable them to live in a "supercooled" state; their body fluids remain liquid at temperatures below the point at which ice forms. Antarctic ice fish (such as the fish on the left) have almost translucent (see-through) blood.

Hair under paws keeps fox from sinking in snow; the fox's Latin name is Alopex lagopus. Lagopus *means "hairy foot"*

Sharp claws to dig through the snow to find food

16

ptarmigan
us mutus

A BIRD FOR ALL SEASONS
A ptarmigan's plumage changes twice
a year so that it is well camouflaged
at all times. Also, the density of its
feathers increases in winter. When
resting overnight, ptarmigans sometimes
burrow in snow to reduce heat loss.

FINE TO BE FAT
Whales and seals are kept warm by a
layer of thick fat called blubber. This
fat walrus is in no danger of getting
cold. Walruses can weigh up to
1.8 tons (1,600 kg), with
tusks 3 ft (1 m) long.

*Ears are furry
inside and out
for extra warmth*

*Dense fur coat with long
hairs traps body warmth*

*Small round ears
and a short muzzle
cut down on heat loss;
foxes from warmer places
have larger ears and a
longer muzzle*

*Sharp, pointed
teeth to grab animals
such as lemmings*

DOUBLE-GLAZED FUR
The Arctic fox's white winter
fur is made up of hairs that
are hollow inside, full
of air. The air in the
hairs traps body
warmth from the
fox in much the
same way as a
double-glazed
window traps
warmth from
houses. Air is a
good insulator and
does not let heat escape
easily. The Arctic fox can tolerate
temperatures of -40°F (-40°C), or
even lower, quite comfortably.

Survival of the fittest

Pale maidens
Sisyrinchium filifolium

Flowers are
both male
and female

Capsules
contain seeds

Plant grows
low to the
ground to
keep out of
the wind

Long roots
obtain
nitrogen
and water
in dry,
harsh
conditions

Root system
anchors plant
firmly in soil

ONLY SPECIALIZED, HARDY PLANTS can survive the fierce winds, biting cold, thin soils, and short growing season of the polar lands. The most successful plants are the simple ones, like mosses, lichens, and algae. Arctic and Antarctic plants often grow in low, compact cushions, called tussocks, to keep out of the freezing, drying winds, to trap available moisture, and to avoid being crushed by snow and ice. In the short summer, flowers burst open and rapidly produce seeds before the winter weather returns. Few insects live in these cold places, so many plants reproduce from small pieces of themselves such as runners or bulbils. The wind may also spread their pollen.

Arctic wormwood
Artemisia borealis

Flower heads are
about 0.25 in
(5–6 mm) across

PALE MAIDENS
This sub-Antarctic plant of the iris family has grasslike leaves. It is able to store food in fleshy roots underground. This ability helps it to survive the cold and dry seasons, and to grow quickly in spring.

SEEDS AWAY
The northern primrose, *Primula scandanavica*, produces many seeds in a capsule. When ripe, the capsule splits open and releases the seeds.

FAST FLOWERS
Calandria feltonii is native only to the Falkland Islands (or Malvinas). A succession of short-lived flowers open quickly when the sun shines.

Fleshy
leaves
store
water

Silky or hairless
leaves are
deeply divided

ARCTIC WORMWOOD
This hardy plant, which grows throughout the northern hemisphere, is sometimes known as Arctic wormwood. It grows in colonies on dry, rocky ridges and gravel banks.

Woolly bear
caterpillar
Arctia caja

...TS OF THE NORTH
...al species of butterflies and
... live in the Arctic regions.
...airs of dark fuzzy
...illars accelerate warming
...duce heat loss.

*Branched
flower head
is called a
panicle*

Northern fleabane
Erigeron borealis

...ranches
...pikelets
...ks

*Daisylike
flowers made
up of small
flowers
called florets*

Slipperwort
Calceolaria fothergillii

*Large lower
petals look
like a slipper*

*Flower sticks
out from leaves
so insects can
spot the flower
easily*

INSECT REPELLENT
Low cushions of northern fleabane bloom
in the Arctic summer, when the tundra
becomes waterlogged and water collects on its
surface. The plant is highly unattractive to fleas
and midges, hence its name, and it is used
successfully by humans as an insect repellent.

...WTH OF GRASS
...ost successful
... in the cold polar
...s are the low-
... mosses and
...s. However,
...al grasses
... in the Arctic,
*...eschampsia
...sa*. On the
...ctic mainland
...ne grass
...ves, *Deschampsia
...sa*, or Antarctic
...-hair grass.

*Hairy leaves
trap warmth
and moisture*

SLIPPERWORT
The rare and beautiful slipperwort grows
along the coasts of the Falkland Islands.
The color of the large, slipper-like lower
petal attracts insects, which helps the plant
to reproduce. When an insect feeds on the
plant's nectar, pollen sticks to its legs and
is carried to another slipper-flower.

TREELESS TUNDRA
The tundra, a vast zone lying between the
ice cap and the timber line of Europe, Asia,
and North America, is the habitat for many
species of plants. The harsh climate and severe
winds dictate that low-lying plants predominate
and there are no trees. To take advantage of the
short summer, some plants complete their
whole life cycle in as little time as possible.

Birds of the Arctic

FEW BIRDS CAN SURVIVE the hostile Arctic climate all yea round, but residents include the ptarmigan, raven, ivor gull, and dovekie. The plumage of Arctic birds is more dense than that of migratory species, especially in the winter. Their feet are protected by feathers and do not freeze to the ice. Most Arctic birds, such as waders, shorebirds, ducks, geese, swans, and gulls, are migrato Some migrants, particularly waders, travel long journe in winter, as far as South America, South Africa, and Australasia. In summer, Arctic birds take advantage of the rich insect and small-mammal life on the tundra, nesting and rapidly rearing young before the win sets in. Many different types of birds can feed and nest in close proximity because they share the available food – for instance, ducks eat wat plants, seabirds eat fish, and waders eat insects

LIKE A BIRD
In 1926, the airship *Norge* carried Norwegian Roald Amundsen and Italian Umberto Nobile over the North Pole.

HAPPY FAMILIES
The dovekie (*Alle alle*) is not much bigger than a thrush, but there are a lot of them! Over 100 million dovekies, or little auks, breed along Arctic coasts each summer. In winter, they move south but usually stay near the Arctic Circle. Dovekies have a thick layer of fat under their skin to keep them warm. They feed on the rich supply of plankton in the sea, storing food in a throat pouch.

Straight, powerful beak for stabbing prey

Long neck to probe in water beds

ON DISPLAY
Cranes mate for life. They perform spectacular courtship dances – head-bobbing, bowing, skipping, and sometimes leaping as high as 20 ft (6 m) in the air.

Streamlined, torpedo-shaped for swimming fast underwa

REDHEADS
Sandhill cranes (*Grus canadensis*) breed mostly in the remote Arctic, laying their eggs in mounds of grass or other plants in an undisturbed marsh. Young birds stay with their parents for nearly a year. The sandhill crane's plumage often appears rusty because of reddish iron oxide stains from the water of tundra ponds. The birds probe with their bills in the mud for worms, water creatures, and frogs, then transfer the stain to their feathers when preening.

BIRD IN THE NET

...ctic birds were an ...uable source of food ...nuit people. Hunters ...a caught the birds in ...ets on long poles.

Moving the two sticks back and forth causes the birds to bob down for their food

TOY TIME

Carving is an ancient Inuit art that often shows Arctic birds and mammals. The villages of Holman Island and Cape Dorset in Canada have become well-known for their style of art. To make this bird-feeding toy work, the two sticks are moved back and forth.

Powerful, slender, dagger-shaped beak to snap up fish and crustaceans

FEATHER BEDS

Eider ducks (*Somateria mollissima*) in the Arctic are migratory, whereas in warmer places they stay near their breeding grounds all year. Eider ducks feed mainly on shellfish, which they swallow whole. Muscles in the bird's stomach crush the shellfish. Eider ducks have particularly soft and dense down feathers for warmth. Female eiders pluck some of their breast feathers to line their nests. People use these feathers to fill quilts.

LOONY BIRDS

Loons, such as this black-throated Arctic loon, are sometimes called divers. Loons are adapted to swimming underwater after their prey, but are clumsy on land because their legs are set so far back on the body. The name loon may come from the Icelandic word *lomr*, meaning lame or clumsy. The Arctic loon breeds on tundra lakes and migrates mainly to the Pacific coast in winter.

Handsome breeding plumage; winter plumage is dull and grayish

WATER LOVERS

Loons spend most of their lives on the water and come on land only to nest. Puffins, too, are excellent swimmers and divers, hunting for shellfish in rocky coastal waters. They are ungainly on land but are able to jump from rock to rock.

Birds of the Antarctic

THE MOST COMMON Antarctic birds are seabirds, such as penguins, albatrosses, and petrels, which come ashore in summer to breed in remote, predator-free locations. They take advantage of the seas around Antarctica, which are pack with food for hungry chicks. Only 13 species of flying birds make use of ice-free land for nesting on the Antarctic mainla▮ The rest squash into colonies on cramped sub-Antarctic islan▮ Antarctic birds rely on their dense feathers and frostbite-resistant feet to keep warm, while fat reserves in the skin act as both food and insulation. Most Antarctic birds lea▮ during the cold winter months. But some, including emperor penguins, king penguins, and wandering albatrosses, stay behind to complet▮ their long breeding cycle. Others, such as sheathbills, only just manage to survive in the freezin▮ winter conditions.

ANTARCTIC SCAVENGERS
` Giant petrels are nicknamed "stinkers" because of their unpleasant smell. They use their powerful hooked beaks for feeding and scavenging, as well as for killing other birds. Petrels will eat almost anything, including dead seals and whales. A petrel is about the size of a vulture, with a wingspan of nearly 6.5 ft (2 m).

Wings are held up like a Viking helmet, making the bird appear large and fierce

Earsplitting shriek warns enemies to keep away

Wings are spread to display white patches

PIRATES OF THE SKIES
Peculiar doglike barking calls signal the arrival of a pair of skuas. Skuas earn their reputation as "pirates of the skies" by chasing other birds and forcing them to regurgitate (bring u▮ their food. These large aggressive b▮ are also notorious for stealing the and young of other birds. Two s▮ may even cooperate while hur▮ using clever tricks to snatch a meal more easily

Powerful hooked beak to stab and kill prey

Antarctic skua
Catharacta maccormicki

Brown skua
Catharacta lonnbergi

NOT FUSSY
Sheathbills are the only land birds that live year-round in Antarctica. Their success is due to their varied diet, which includes penguin and seal feces, penguin eggs, chicks, dead fish, krill, and limpets. Sheathbills also steal food intended for penguin chicks.

Horny sheath protects nostrils

Orange growths at base of beak become brighter during breeding season

Jagged, hooked bill helps to grip slippery fish

Blue-eyed cormorant
Phalacrocorax atriceps

...gs are spread out ...y off after a swim

Feathers soak up water and allow the cormorant to dive more easily

Tern
Albatross
Shearwater
Cormorant
Penguin

DIFFERENT STROKES
The pursuit of a fishy meal involves a different technique for every type of bird. Cormorants use their strong feet to paddle deep underwater after prey; penguins dive deep, then propel themselves through the sea using their wings. A tern picks fish by plunging down just under the surface of the water, and albatrosses float on the surface, keeping a sharp eye out for any possible food. Shearwaters spot their prey from the air and then plunge in pursuit.

SEAWEED NEST
Blue-eyed cormorants nest in smelly, noisy colonies close to the sea, building untidy nests of seaweed, lichens, mosses, and feathers glued together with guano (bird excrement). Blue-eyed cormorants breed on the Antarctic peninsula and on a number of Antarctic and sub-Antarctic islands. Some use their nesting sites all year round, roosting there throughout the winter. This allows them to stay near their fishing grounds in open water.

Snowy owl
Nyctea scandiaca

Lords of the skies

THE HUGE SUMMER BREEDING COLONIES of birds in both the Arctic and the Antarctic attract a number of predatory birds quick to enjoy the easy meals of eggs and chicks. In the Arctic, the small mammals of the tundra lands, such as lemmings and hares, increase the range of food for birds to hunt. The variety of predatory birds is therefore greater in the Arctic than in the Antarctic, and includes eagles, skuas, owls, falcons, and buzzards. The predators time their own breeding cycle to coincide with that of their prey, to ensure that their chicks will always have plenty to eat.

GHOSTLY HUNTER
Snowy owls feed primarily on the millions of lemmings living on the Arctic tundra. Owl population usually follows the rise and fall of the lemming population on its three- to four-year cycle (pp. 36–37). Many of these owls wander far south in winter.

Soapstone and ivory owl carved by Inuit craftsman in Cape Dorset, Canada

Feathers at tips of wings spread out like fingers to help the eagle push and steer through the air

Spread feathers help the bird to reduce speed

Lethal curved talons grip, crush, and carry off prey

Strong legs to cushion impact of landing

The golden eagle slows in midair and spreads out its wings and tail to act as a brake

Eyes focused firmly on its destination, the eagle further brakes its flight by swinging out its lower body and legs

At the last moment, its feet swing down to grip the perch

WATCH OUT BEL
Golden eagles fly at altitudes while hunt then swoop sudden pounce on their prey. swoop-and-grab at is effective becau happens so swiftly the prey is often take surprise. Here, a go eagle is landing branch in much the s way as it would w diving for a m

24

KING OF THE CLOUDS
As the most powerful and majestic bird in the sky, the eagle features in countless stories, myths, and legends. In this illustration by British artist Reginald Knowles, a magnificent eagle perches in a tree. It appears on the title page of a collection of Norse legends.

Golden eagle
Aquila chrysaetos

Keen eyesight to spot birds and animals moving on the ground below

ful hooked
tear flesh
rey

Huge chest muscles drive the enormous wings

Gyrfalcon
Falco rusticolus

ers
to toes
p warm

BIGGEST AND BEST
The gyrfalcon, most powerful of the falcons, relies on power and speed to catch its victims. They usually kill their prey in flight.

LLING MACHINE
agnificent flier, the golden eagle is
rce predator of ptarmigan and other
s, as well as small mammals such as
nd squirrels and hares. Golden eagles
lly kill their prey before carrying it
their strong talons. They sometimes
in pairs, especially in winter.

FALCON FOOD
The rock ptarmigan (*Lagopus mutus*) is the gyrfalcon's main prey.

Ocean wanderer

THE HUGE, GENTLE ALBATROSSES of the Antarctic seas come ashore only to breed. They do not breed on the Antarctic land mass itself but on islands such as South Georgia, just north of the pack ice. There are six species of albatross that breed in the Antarctic: the black-browed, gray-headed, yellow-nosed, wandering, sooty, and light-mantled sooty. Probably about 750,000 pairs of birds breed each year. The main advantage of these isolated locations is safety from predators. Albatrosses raise only one chick at a time. The chick takes a long time to mature, sometimes remaining in the nest for up to a year. Chicks are protected from the intense cold by thick down feathers and an insulating layer of blubber, or fat. When winter begins, most albatrosses set off over the southern oceans once more.

DEAD WEIGHT
Sailors believed albatrosses brought them good luck. In Coleridge's *The Rime of the Ancient Mariner*, the unlucky mariner is forced to wear an albatross he has killed.

Black-browed albatross
Diomedea melanophris

Webbed feet held wide to push against the air and act as brakes

BUMPY LANDING
Landing is a difficult task for a bird so well adapted to flying over the sea. When albatrosses approach the nest site, they circle around several times before putting their legs down, like the landing gear on an aircraft. But they often land with a bump.

Gray-headed albatross
Diomedea chrysostoma

Large eyes indicate sharp eyesight necessary for spotting food in the sea

BIRD MAN
People have always wanted to fly like birds, but this design an early flying machine was no challenge to the albatross mastery of the air. For birds, like airplanes, takeoff an landing are the most dangerous parts of flying. Because of their enormous wingspan and body weight, albatrosses also need a runway to gather enough speed for takeoff.

Tube-shaped nostrils have glands at the base that excrete excess salt

Bill has razor-sharp edges to catch fish and squid

LIVING THE HIGH LIFE
Although gray-headed albatrosses weigh only half as much as wandering albatrosses, they still find it hard to take off, so they live on steep cliff sides and get extra lift from the strong winds rising up over the cliffs. Because of the harsh conditions, only half their chicks survive, a rate which is not unusually low for Antarctic birds.

During courtship the bird points its beak to the sky and moos like a cow

...ONDHAND FOOD
...nt albatrosses feed their young by
...rgitating (bringing up) the food
...eat, in the form of a sticky, oily
...ure. This feeding takes place
...n they return to the nest after
...y hours, or even days, of fishing
...at sea. Both adults and young
...use this smelly and sticky
...or defense, ejecting it with
...onable accuracy over a six-
...(2 m) range. Predators, such
...uas, may be repelled by the
...smell or immobilized if the
...y oil saturates their feathers.

*...her feeds
...rgitated
...to chick*

Nest is lined with grass and feathers

Nest is about 12 in (30 cm) high

...RREL NEST
...e black-browed albatross makes
...ised nest of mud and straw
...ong the tussock grass.

FAITHFUL FLYING ACE
The wandering albatross has the greatest wingspan of any living bird. Its wing power enables the bird to cover over 300 miles (500 km) a day, alighting on the sea to feed in calm weather. Like all albatrosses, it comes ashore only to breed. The breeding cycle is exceptionally long, taking a year to complete. It therefore breeds only every two years. Breeding is preceded by an elaborate courtship display, in which the two birds dance face to face, making a variety of sounds and clapping their beaks together loudly. Wandering albatrosses usually pair for life. The most elaborate displays take place among newly formed pairs; old established partners are more discreet.

Wingspan may be between 8 ft 4 in–11 ft 10 in (254–360 cm)

Wandering albatross
Diomedea exulans

Strong legs and wide feet assist landing and swimming

South Pole penguins

ONE OF THE MOST SPECTACULAR SIGHTS of the Antarctic is the millions of penguins gathered at their noisy summer breeding colonies. Only two species, the Adélie and the emperor, breed on the Antarctic continent itself, but the gentoo, macaroni, chinstrap, rockhopper, and king penguins all breed within Antarctic waters. Emperor and king penguins lay a single egg each year; the other species usually lay two eggs. Penguins are supremely well adapted for swimming in cold seas. Some of these adaptations, particularly the dense, waterproof feathers and thick fat layers under the skin, also serve them well on land. The penguins rely on the fat as an energy supply when they are caring for eggs and chicks and cannot get out to sea to obtain food for themselves.

Short beak has feathers along part of its length for extra warmth

SAFETY IN NUMBERS
Penguins breed in huge, densely packed colonies called rookeries. Some rookeries contain millions of birds.

A PRACTICAL PENGUIN
Adélies winter out at sea off the pack ice but march inland to their breeding colonies in October. They navigate partly by means of the sun. Adélies usually return to the same mates and nest sites every year. They lay eggs in November and by February the chicks go to sea.

Powerful oarlike flippers propel penguins through water

Stiff tail of pointed feathers used as rudder in water and as support on land

Torpedo-shaped body allows the penguin to slice through the water

Oily feathers overlap like roof tiles, providing a waterproof layer for the thick down feathers underneath

PERFIDIOUS PENGUIN
An evil penguin stars in the Oscar-winning British animated film *The Wrong Trousers*. The treacherous penguin leaves a trail of havoc behind it as it attempts to remove a priceless jewel from a museum. Penguins are not, however, generally famed for their participation in diamond heists!

Adélie penguin
Pygoscelis adeliae

Short legs are set far back on body for steering while swimming

PADDED PENGUINS PARASCENDING
Tough feathers, a flexible skin, and thick blubber protect these penguins from knocks as they hurl themselves onto rocky shores or ice floes.

King penguin
*Aptenodytes
patagonica*

MARK OF DISTINCTION
The main distinguishing
marks of penguins are
on the head and upper
breast, so the birds are
visible when they swim
on the surface. The
colors and head crests
are used for species
recognition and for
courtship displays.

Gentoo penguin
Pygoscelis papua

Rockhopper penguin
*Eudyptes
chrysocome*

KING PENGUINS
Kings have golden-orange
patches on their ears and bill.
The long bill is useful for
catching speedy fish and squid.

GENTOO PENGUINS
The pink bill of gentoos is dagger-
shaped to catch fish and krill.
Gentoos can swim at speeds of
up to 16 miles (27 km) per hour.

ROCKHOPPER PENGUINS
Rockhoppers have conspicuous
yellow eyebrows that they use for
courtship display. They are the
smallest polar penguin.

NOISY NESTERS
Chinstrap penguins are good
climbers, using their beaks and
sharp claws to reach nest sites
in high rocky places. They are
noisy and aggressive penguins.
They often take over the
nesting sites of Adélies or
steal stones from one
another's nests.

black feathers
form a
"chinstrap"
across
white
breast

CHICKS AT RISK
Weak and sickly chicks,
or those on the edge of the
colonies, are most likely to fall
victim to predators such as
the skua (right). In the
oceans, penguins
are prey to
leopard seals,
sea lions, and
killer whales.

shallow
nest
lined with
stones and
vegetation

Chinstrap
penguin
*Pygoscelis
antarctica*

Emperors of the Antarctic

In EARLY APRIL, when most of Antarctica's wildlife heads north, the emperor penguin begins its 60-mile (100-km) trek south to its traditional nesting sites on the sea ice. To reach the breeding colony, the birds must cover a huge area of sea ice in pitch darkness. In early May the female lays her egg and returns north to the open sea. The male then undertakes an incredible feat of endurance. During the icy winter he incubates the egg on his feet under a flap of warm skin. This means that for two months the male cannot feed, and may lose up to half his body weight. The female returns to feed the hatched chick in July. Each pair of emperors rears one chick a year, but only about one out of five survives.

FEET HEAT
Chicks stand on the adults' feet until they are about eight weeks old, hiding under a brood pouch, or flap of skin, for extra warmth and protection. Older chicks rely on their dense, fluffy feathers and the warm bodies of fellow chicks to keep them warm while their parents search for food.

TRULY MAJESTIC
The emperor, the largest penguin, stands nearly 4 ft (1.2 m) tall, and weighs 65 lb (30 kg). It can spend up to 18 minutes underwater and dive to over 850 ft (260 m).

The birds in the center are the warmest of the group

A tightly packed group can reduce heat loss by as much as 50 percent

Any bird that fails to join the huddle during the winter months faces certain death

Birds take turns occupying the most exposed positions

Emperors tend to turn their backs on the constantly shifting wind

TOGETHERNESS
Incubating males huddle together for warmth, moving very little in order to conserve energy. When the chicks are born the birds still huddle together as much as possible. Some emperor colonies contain over 20,000 pairs.

After the females return, the skinny and hungry males make their way to the open sea

Penguin "flies" out of the water to draw breath

Penguin catches fish and krill in its beak

Underwater, penguin steers with its feet and tail

Penguin shoots onto land or ice in giant leap of up to 6 ft (2 m)

DUCKING AND DIVING
Penguins "fly" through the water, propelled by their stiff flippers. When swimming fast, they often use a technique called porpoising, leaping out of the water like dolphins or porpoises. Air offers less resistance to movement than water, so porpoising penguins can travel at speeds of 18 miles (30 km) an hour.

Bill is small to cut
down on heat loss

Emperor penguin
Aptenodytes forsteri

In the nasal
cavities, much of
the warm air
that would
otherwise be lost
in breathing is
recycled

Closely packed,
overlapping
feathers cover a
thick layer of
blubber

Feet are small
to cut down on
heat loss

King of the Arctic

THE POLAR BEAR IS THE LARGEST and most powerful hunter of the Arctic lands; an average male weighs as much as six adult people. There are probably 20,000 polar bears wandering over the vast Arctic ice floes; some of them even roam as far as the North Pole. Polar bears are solitary animals except in the breeding season. They do not hibernate, and in the long winter, when the Arctic pack ice extends farther out to sea, they hunt for seals beneath the ice. Their dense fur keeps them warm even in the most severe conditions. An undercoat of thick fur is protected by an outer coat of long guard hairs. These hairs stick together when they get wet, forming a waterproof barrier. Under the fur, a thick layer of blubber performs two roles, insulating the bear against the cold and acting as a food store to help the bear survive hard times.

The small rounded ears lose little body heat

HEAVYWEIGHT
An average adult male polar bear measures 8 ft (2.5 m) from head to tail and weighs over 1,000 lb (about 500 kg). The largest males grow up to 10 ft (3 m) in length and can weigh up to 2,000 lb (900 kg). Female polar bears are much smaller than the males.

Female keeps floor clean by covering it with freshly scraped snow

Air vent scraped in roof lets stale air escape

Female first digs the tunnel, then hollows out the chamber

CAPABLE CLIMBER
In spite of their huge size, polar bears are able to climb trees, such as this one at Cape Churchill on Hudson Bay in Canada. Between 600 and 1,000 bears gather here in October to wait for the bay to freeze over so that they can head out over the ice to hunt.

Thick fur prevents bear from being scratched

Back legs are especially strong

Strong teeth for killing prey

BEARING ARMS
By playing, cubs gain strength and practice skills they will need when they are adults. Young bears often wrestle in the snow with their mouths wide open to show off their sharp teeth. Such fights rarely result in injury. Finding and killing prey is not easy, and bears have developed a bad reputation for raiding human settlements in search of food.

CAVE CUBS
Polar bear cubs are born in December or January in a warm cozy den dug in the snow by the mother. The cubs grow rapidly on their mother's rich milk, which is about 30 percent fat. While in the ice cave, the mother has nothing to eat and lives on the stored fat in her body.

r bears are slow but very
g swimmers, able to keep
wimming for a long time.
bears use only their front
egs to propel themselves;
he back legs are held still
like a rudder.

SEAL SLAYER
Polar bears are clever and patient
hunters. Over 90 percent of their
diet consists of seals. They
wait by a seal's blowhole
in the ice, pouncing as
soon as it comes up for
air. One stroke of the
bear's massive paw and
a bite at the back of the skull
kill the seal. But most hunting
trips are unsuccessful, and a bear
may not eat for five days.

*Yellow-white fur
acts as camouflage*

*Powerful legs
to outrun prey*

*Hollow hairs
trap warm air
near body*

*Thickly padded soles
covered by rough skin and
sometimes tough hair*

*Sharp claws for
grabbing prey*

*Non-slip soles help
grip slippery ice*

Flat shape gives moose a stable surface with which to push rivals

The bell is a fold of skin covered with hair

The mighty moose

THE MOOSE IS THE LARGEST MEMBER of the deer family. It stands up to 7.5 ft (2.4 m) tall and can weigh up to 1,800 lb (825 kg). The moose can be found throughout the northern United States and Canada, and in northern Europe and Asia, where it is sometimes called elk. In Europe and Asia the moose lives mainly in the coniferous forests bordering the tundra, but in North America it ranges widely over the tundra, spending long periods on the shores of the Arctic ocean in midsummer, when flies are likely to plague it farther inland. When winters are particularly harsh, moose often move farther south in search of food, to areas that have lighter snow cover. Moose are solitary animals and their population density is low; because of their immense size they need a relatively large area to themselves to enable them to find an adequate food supply. However, in winter, when in search of new food supplies, they will often travel in a group, covering considerable distances.

LETHAL WEAPONS
The bull moose has heavy, flat antlers. It uses them more for fighting rival males during the breeding season than for protection. The moose sheds its antlers every year and grows a new set. By late August the antlers are fully grown, and the bull strips off the "velvet" covering and polishes his great weapons against a tree.

Undersurface of moose's foot

SURE-FOOTED
The moose has long and sharply pointed hooves, in contrast to those of its relative, the reindeer, which are rounded. The pointed hooves help the moose grip ice and snow.

Moose
Alces alces

Calf remains close to mother for several months

Reddish-brown coat becomes darker as the calf matures

Long legs allow even young moose to walk easily through deep snow

MAKING MORE MOOSE
The mating season of the moose lasts from four to eight weeks in the fall. The bull wanders around looking for and calling to females (cows); the cow return the calls. The bull will follow every sound to see if it was made by a cow or a rival bull. Baby moose are born in late May and June. The mother carries the baby for about seven and a half months before the birth. There is usually one calf, although twins and even triplets are not uncommon. Wh the calf is about ten days old, it travel with its mother.

*Antler spread can be as
much as 6 ft 8 in (2.05 m)*

*Antlers are not
fully grown and
are still heavily
covered with velvet*

MONEY MOOSE
The moose is such a revered
animal in many northern
European countries that it
has even been featured on
banknotes. This note
comes from Lithuania.

*e
3–4 in
cm) over
n*

*Short neck, coupled
with long legs,
means that moose
has to get on its
knees to eat low-
growing plants*

SOLITARY GIANT
The preferred habitat of moose
is tundra land containing willow
swamps and lakes. Moose are good
swimmers and can cross lakes and
rivers with ease. They like to roll in mud
holes, which helps them to get rid of any
small parasitic animals. In summer, they eat
leaves and tender twigs as well as grass
and herbs. Because of their great size and
dangerous antlers they have few natural
predators, with the exception of humans.
Wolves may occasionally attack isolated
moose and the young, although the antlers
of the adult make it a formidable foe.

Arctic
willow
*Salix
arctica*

ORITE FOOD
tic willow (*Salix arctica*) and
ska willow (*Salix alaxensis*) are
favorite foods of the moose.

*Moose is beginning to lose
the velvet on its antlers*

WATER WADERS
Moose are often to be found standing up to their knees in
water. This helps them to get rid of the flies that trouble
them greatly in the warm summer months, but they also
ed on the aquatic vegetation. An adult will consume up to
43 lb (19.5 kg) of vegetation a day. Sometimes they retreat
into water to escape predators such as wolves.

Tundra wildlife

TUNDRA VEGETATION
The tundra consists of a nearly continuous, though at times thin, cover of vegetation, dominated by grasses like the Arctic cottongrass (*Eriophorum angustifolium*) seen here. Scattered among the grasses are various mosses, a variety of flowering herbs, and a few species of dwarf shrubs and willows.

THE ONLY ANIMAL that can live on the Arctic pack ice is the polar bear. However, several animals live on the Arctic tundra (pp. 8–9), both as residents and migrants. During summer in the Arctic a great deal of the ice on the tundra melts, plants begin to flourish, and insect eggs hatch. This means that suddenly there is plenty of food for animals that have spent all winter on the tundra, as well as for the migrants who arrive as soon as the snows melt. Because the sun never sets in the Arctic in summer (pp. 6–7), the animals can feed all through the night. It is necessary for them to do this so that the young can grow as quickly as possible, because the summer is short and the land soon freezes over again.

Limit of permanent ice
Limit of drift ice
Tree line
Tundra

Canada
Arctic Circle
Arctic Ocean
Greenland
Rus

SEA OF ICE
The central area of the Arctic O remains permanently frozen. T tundra, which spans North An and Eurasia, is covered in snow ice in winter but is green in summer. No trees grow on the tundra because it is too cold an windy, even in the summer mo

Long, pointed ears enable the lynx to hear well in dense, muffling snow

FELINE VISITOR
The Arctic lynx (*Lynx canadensis*) is mainly a creature of the forest that borders areas of the tundra in North America, but they are often found in the true tundra during the summer months. Their brown coat blends well with the tundra landscape in summer, and in winter the coat becomes thicker and lighter so that the lynx is hard to see against the snow.

Snowshoe hare
Lepus americanus

The lemming is a common on the t

HARE LINE
Three types of hares inhabit the tundra – the snowshoe hare, the rare Alaskan hare, and the common Arctic hare. Hares grow white winter coats and have well-developed claws that enable them to dig through the snow for food.

MASS SUICIDE?
Every few years, when their numbers outgrow their food so lemmings (*Lemmus sibiricus*) be restless and a mass migration begins. They press on madly, c passing food sources, until the reach the sea, where hundreds drown.

In winter big feet are covered with thick fur that acts like a snowshoe

TURNCOAT
The stoat (*Mustela erminea*) is protected from harsh weather in its home beneath the snow. It is often called "ermine" when its coat is in its white win phase. It is a cute-looking animal, but a ruthless hunter. The stoat's slimness enables it to pursu lemmings, its main prey, through the lemming networks of underground tunnels.

GREAT BEAR

The word "Arctic" comes from the Greek word *Arctikos*, meaning "pertaining to the constellation of the bear." The extensive star constellation Ursa Major, the Great Bear, is visible only in the northern hemisphere.

GLUTTON OF THE ARCTIC

The wolverine (*Gulo gulo*), a distant relative of the stoat, looks like a small bear. Wolverines are solitary animals and usually meet others only to mate during the summer. They are relentless hunters, able to pursue their victims for many miles without tiring. Their main prey is reindeer. After a kill, much of the flesh is eaten on the spot, but they hide the remainder for another day, earning themselves a reputation for gluttony. Wolverine fur is much prized.

Sometimes the fur is tipped silvery white

...have ...ive noses ...strong ...of smell

...owerful jaws and ...eth allow bear to ...t a variety of foods

...PYHEAD

...rown or grizzly bear ...s arctos) lives in the ...ra regions of Alaska and ...da and in some parts of ...a. They eat a wide variety of ...mammals, fish, insects, and ...s, depending on the season and ...rea in which they live. In the ...r months the grizzly digs a snug ...n the ground and hibernates, taking ...oximately two weeks to enter a deep ...r sleep. During hibernation the body ...erature drops and the bear lives off its ...ves of stored fat. It sometimes sleeps for ...g as seven months.

Long claws on the front paws help the bear to dig

Bears often stand upright on the soles of their back feet

37

Reindeer and caribou

REINDEER ARE CALLED CARIBOU in North America. The name "caribou" may come from *xalibu*, the Native American Micmac word for "the animal that paws through snow for its food." Wild reindeer still survive on the frozen tundra of North America, Siberia, and Scandinavia, but they have also been domesticated in Scandinavia and Siberia for thousands of years. Although their thick coats insulate them against the Arctic cold, they migrate south in the winter to find food and shelter. As they travel, their coats grow thick and gray. In summer, reindeer are plagued by hordes of insects, such as mosquitoes and warble flies, as they graze on the tundra meadows. Their main predator is the wolf; this natural population regulation is necessary to enable the surviving reindeer to find sufficient food in a decreasing habitat.

REINDEER STAR
The most famous reindeer in the world is probably red-nosed Rudolph, the reindeer who leads Santa Claus's sleigh.

TITLE FIGHT
In the fall rutting, or mating, season, bulls with their antlers locked together wrestle to decide which is the strongest. The winner of these contests collects a group of cows for mating and then defends his harem from all challenges.

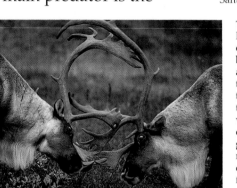

Antler buds appear two weeks after the old ones are shed

New antlers are covered by soft, thick velvet

Fully formed antlers are bone-hard

BIG, BIGGER, BIGGEST
Antlers are shed each year. Bulls shed their antlers at the end of the year, but the cows wait until spring. New antlers grow rapidly and are fully grown by the start of the fall rutting season.

Nuclear explosion

NUCLEAR POLLUTION
In 1986 a nuclear reactor at Chernobyl in Ukraine exploded. Lichens and mosses absorbed radioactive Cesium 137. Reindeer ate the lichens, making them ill and their meat unfit to eat.

Reindeer moss (*Cladonia* species) absorbed radioactivity from the air

Velvet contains blood vessels to nourish the growing antlers

LICHEN LUNCH
Reindeer feed largely on lichens, which are one of the few foods available throughout the Arctic winter. Some reindeer living on Arctic islands will also eat seaweed. In summer a wider variety of plants are available. Adult reindeer eat about 10 lb (4.5 kg) of food a day to get the energy they need.

Reindeer, or caribou
Rangifer tarandus

Sensitive nose helps reindeer to find food even under the snow

CEREMONIAL APRON

This shaman's ceremonial apron was made from reindeer hide. The shaman was a powerful figure in the culture of many native Siberian and North American peoples. It was believed he could get power from supernatural beings that were everywhere on land, and even lurked beneath the sea.

Iron symbols of the sun, fish, and diving birds decorate apron

Heat is lost rapidly through antlers in velvet, cooling the reindeer on hot summer days

Hollow hairs contain air that traps body heat

SWIMMING CHAMPIONS

Migrating reindeer have to cross many fast-flowing rivers. They are strong swimmers, plunging into the icy waters without any hesitation. The reindeers' broad feet help them to swim against the current, and the hollow hairs in their coats help them to float more easily.

Iron-bladed reindeer skin scraper used by Siberian Tungus tribe

Lapp stick with spade-like blade to probe under the snow for food

TOOLS OF THE TRADE

Many Scandinavian and Siberian peoples relied on the reindeer for food, clothing, and shelter. They devised many tools specifically to enable them to take full advantage of their domesticated animals.

Muzzle covered with fine, warm hair

Dense, waterproof coat turns gray-white in winter

Sharp hooves grip ice and dig through snow for food

*d feet
ed
fur
reindeer
sinking
now*

GROWING UP FAST

Calves are born in June and grow fast on their mothers' rich milk, which is four times as nutritious as cow's milk. Calves can keep up with the movements of the herd when they are one or two days old, and are better protected from predators such as wolves if they remain within its safety. Calves stay with their mothers for about a year, growing their first antlers when they are around two months old.

Company of wolves

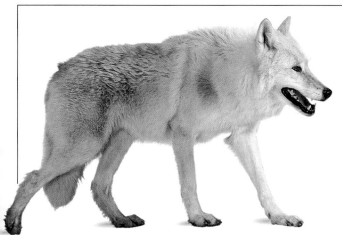

BLENDING INTO THE BACKGROUND
In the Arctic areas of North America and Eurasia, wolves often have white coats for camouflage. Because the animals they hunt cannot see them easily, the wolves can get very close to their prey. In the forests to the south of the tundra, the wolves have gray or even blackish fur.

WOLVES ARE INTELLIGENT AND ADAPTABLE animals that survive in the Arctic cold thanks to their thic fur and cooperative hunting techniques. They generally live in packs of between 8 and 20 famil members. They are bonded together by affection for each other, and by a ranking system of near-military precision. Pack members establish their rank at almost every meeting: a dominant or high ranking wolf stands erect, ears and tail pointing upward, and may show its teeth, then growl. A subordinate or low-ranking wolf crouches, holds its tail between its legs, and turns down its ears; instead of growling, it whines. A wolf pack rang over a specific area, picking off sick, aged, or injured herd animals. Needlessly feared and persecuted by humans for thousands of years, wolves kill only to survive, and do not deserve their bad reputation – they are, in fact, the ancestors of all domesticated dogs.

RING OF HORN
Wolves are expert hunters and prey chiefly on large hooved animals such as caribou, moose, and musk oxen. To defend themselves from a wolf pack, a herd of musk oxen forms a tight circle, with the wolves on the outside and the females and young in the center. By panicking the musk oxen, the wolves can break the circle and reach the calves inside. But if a wolf is caught by one of the musk oxen's horns, it can be tossed into the air and then trampled.

Mouth remains wide open during howling

Wolf throws back its head in order to howl

Wolf
Canis lupus

IN HARMONY
An eerie howl in the night echoes through countless horror films, striking terror into the hearts of the audience. In fact, howling is simply one of the ways in which wolves communicate with one another. Wolf-speak ranges from whimpers and growls to complex facial and body expressions. Wolves howl in order to keep in touch with pack members, or to warn other packs to keep out of the area. If one wolf howls, the others join in, often harmonizing with each other. The variety of sound makes the pack seem bigger and more formidable.

LEADER OF THE PACK
The wolf's instinct for power an freedom has inspired countless wr The American novelist Jack Lond wrote his novel *The Call of the Wild* spending a year in the Yukon i Canada. It is the story of Buck, domestic dog who becomes wild eventually leads a wolf pack.

Sensitive ears can track sounds
up to 2 miles (3 km) away

Wolves have as
many as 17
different facial
expressions

Poor eyesight means wolves
must rely on superb hearing
and sense of smell

ong muzzle hides powerful jaws
d teeth for killing prey and
aring flesh; 42 teeth include
arp canines for gripping prey

vo-layered coat with soft,
nse underfur and long outer
airs to keep out the cold

THE WOLF WITHIN
Jack London's novel *White Fang*,
set in the Yukon Territory, is
the story of a wolf domesticated
to become a pet. In practice, it
is virtually impossible – and
illegal – to keep wild
wolves as pets.

N TO BE WILD
ves are superbly adapted to Arctic life.
keen sense of smell and hearing has
honed to perfection for tracking down
prey. They have evolved strong bodies
ong legs for chasing their quarry. Agile
graceful, they can jump up to 15 ft
n) and can leap upward, sideways,
even backward, like a cat. Just like dogs,
es walk on their toes and have large
with claws that do not retract. This
vs them to run fast on flat ground while
ing their footing on rocks, ice, and other
very surfaces.

es can sleep out in the
tundra, although they
find a snow hole or a
in which to shelter

wolf
s lupus

The weighty walrus

HUGE, UNGAINLY, AND ENORMOUSLY FAT, the walrus, a clos relative of the seal, has adapted superbly to its Arctic lifesty A thick layer of blubber (fat) keeps the animal warm. Its fou flat flippers make the walrus an excellent swimmer, as well allowing it to shift its heavy bulk on land. Female walruses give birth in the spring, usually on boulder-strewn beaches. The female usually produces one calf every other year, and cares for her young for about two years – twins are very rar Walruses follow the seasonal ebb and flow of the Arctic ice, migrating as far as 1,800 miles (3,000 km) north each year. I the process, the animals must evade polar bears and killer whales, their greatest enemies other than humans.

WORLD-FAMOUS WALRUS
Lewis Carroll (1832–98)
included a walrus and a
carpenter in his famous story
Alice Through the Looking Glass. They
invite some oysters to walk with them –
and then eat them. In real life, walruses do eat
mainly shellfish, such as clams and mussels.

THE CALL OF LOVE
Walrus courtship is an elaborate process. A
male seduces a female with barks, growls,
and whistles. If she is impressed by his
love song, she will slip off with him
and mate in the water. These two
walruses are tenderly rubbing
mustaches prior to mating.

*Thick skin on neck an
shoulders protects the
walrus during fights*

FURRY FRIEND
Just like the much smaller catfish,
walruses have a row of coarse but
very sensitive whiskers. The
whiskers grow constantly
to make up for daily
wear and tear. The
walrus uses the
delicate mustache
to search for
invertebrates
on the murky
ocean floor.

*Broad front flippers
can support heavy
body on land*

Walrus
Odobenus rosmarus

HEAVYWEIGHT
Weighing in at
around 2,200 lb
(1 tonne), this
formidable male
walrus surveys his
domain. Females are
only slightly smaller,
weighing about 1,900
lb (0.85 tonne).

AN INTIMATE ARRANGEMENT
Walruses are extremely sociable animals. During the
summer, enormous groups of walruses lie around on the
land, packed together in large, noisy groups. Keeping close
together conserves body heat, as well as making it harder
for a predator to pick off an individual animal.

Carved animals
decorate the tusk

Cribbage game board
carved from a walrus tusk

*Walrus ivory is harder
than elephant ivory*

[MUL]TIPURPOSE ANIMAL

[This] cribbage board was probably
[mad]e by a European sailor, but
[th]e Inuit people of North
[Ame]rica have also always hunted
[walr]uses. They, too, carve and
[deco]rate the tusks, but they also eat
[the m]eat, use the hides for shelter or
[to m]ake boats, and burn the blubber
[fo]r heat and light.

[HEA]VE HO!

[Duri]ng the winter and spring,
[walr]uses spend much of their time
[float]ing along on large floating fields
[of ic]e. They use their tusks as ice picks
[to he]ave themselves out of the water,
[flop]ping belly down onto the ice.

*Heavy skull protects
brain when animal
smashes though ice
up to 9 in (22 cm) thick*

*Thin layer of body hair is
molted (shed) every summer*

*Blubber may be more
than 4 in (10 cm) thick*

LONG IN THE TOOTH

A walrus's tusks are actually
its upper canine teeth, and
they may grow as long as 3 ft
(1 m). The walrus perhaps
uses its tusks to rake up the
sea floor in the search for food.
Walruses do not attack humans,
but an angry, wounded walrus
can injure a hunter and damage
his boat when thrashing its
head about.

Lower jaw

*Walrus can
stab larger
prey with its
tusks, but it
eats mainly
shellfish*

Suited to the sea

SEALS ARE PROBABLY the hardiest of all the Arctic and Antarctic mammals. The ringed seal of the Arctic and the Weddell seal of the Antarctic both survive below the ice during the dark winter months. Other seals, such as the Arctic harp seal, migrate into polar waters as the warmer summer weather arrives. All seals have to leave the water to rest, give birth, and mate. In contrast to their graceful swimming in the sea, seals move clumsily on land, wriggling and sliding across the ice with some difficulty. Seals usually give birth in late winter. By spring the pups are strong enough to start making the most of the fish and rich food supplies of the polar waters. Fur seals and sea lions have problems coping with the heat of an Arctic or Antarctic summer. Their fur and blubber causes them to overheat, and the seals have to pant, flap their flippers, or cover their bodies with sand or mud to cool down. Seals have been hunted for their fur and blubber for hundreds of years; they are also threatened by the increasing pollution of the oceans.

Guard hairs protect the seal as it slides over rocks on land

Dense underfur traps a layer of warm air and keeps seal warm

TWO FUR COATS
Fur seals have two kinds of hair in their coat. Long gua[rd] hairs on the outside form a protective layer, and fine underfur keeps body heat from escaping. Other seals h[ave] hairless bodies, and depend on their blubber for warm[th]

ICY WINTERS
Weddell seals (*Leptonychotes weddelli*) spend the who[le] winter under the Antarctic ice sheet, gnawing at the i[ce] with their teeth to keep air holes open for breathing. [In] summer, the seals move onto the ice or rocks. Pups a[re] born in September or October, and can swim at abou[t] six weeks. Weddell seals make a wide range of soun[ds] underwater, possibly for locating prey or blowholes, to communicate with other seals. They can dive to depths of about 1,900 ft (580 m), and stay submerge[d] for up to 70 minutes.

BALLOON NOSE
Male hooded seals (*Cystaphora cristata*) have an inflatable balloon-like structure at the end of their nose. It is blown up when the seal is excited or in danger, and may serve to warn off rivals or enemies.

The male has a huge swollen nose like an elephant's trunk

JOBS FOR THE BOYS
Gigantic male southern elephant seals (*Mirounga leonina*) roar defiance [at] their rivals in the breeding season, usin[g] their extraordinary n[ose] like a loudspeaker. Th[e] female gives birth to a single pup, which she nurses for about a mont[h.] During this period she wi[ll] not feed, existing instead on energy reserves in her blubber. Males do not eat during the breedi[ng] season either, since they are constan[tly] defending a harem of females again[st] rival males.

Male elephant seals are up to ten times heavier than females

While it is nursed the pup may quadruple its weight in three to four weeks.

HIDDEN DEATH
Inuit hunters sometimes hide behind white shields mounted [on] small sleds as they hunt seals

**...s on
...k teeth
...r food**

Cranium

...ENT TEETH
...rabeater seal (*Lobodon
...ophagus*) does not eat crabs.
...s its trident-shaped teeth
...ain shrimplike krill from
...ctic waters. The crabeater
...s at great speed with its mouth
...forcing the water through
...s in its teeth. Between five
...ight million crabeater seals
...n the Antarctic; they have few
...ies, other than killer whales.

*Huge mouth can gape
wide open and snap
shut to grasp prey*

*...erful canine teeth
...ripping flesh*

BUILT FOR A PURPOSE
A seal limb looks very
different from a human
foot. Under the skin,
however, the bones are
the same, adapted over
millions of years to their
different functions. A seal
limb has been modified to
form a webbed paddle.
True seals use their back
flippers to swim through
the water; fur seals and
sea lions use their
front flippers instead,
keeping the back
flippers as a rudder
for steering.

Fibula

*Lower leg
bones*

Tibia

*Ankle
bone*

Ankle bone

Foot bones

*Sole
bones*

Toe bones

Toe bones

Seal flipper

Human foot

*Large eyes
to find prey
underwater*

SEAL THERAPY
When the strains of underwater life become
too much, most seals, such as this leopard
seal, hoist themselves up onto the ice for
a rest and some sunbathing.

...TTED HUNTER
...aggressive leopard seal
...*drurga leptonyx)* is named for the
...e dark spots on its skin. These
...der animals are built for speed,
...have a long, flexible neck and a
...e mouth for grasping penguins,
...pups, and other prey. Leopard
...s pursue penguins underwater,
...carry their victims to the
...face, where they beat them against
...water, turning them inside out to
...ove the skin, before gulping them
...wn. The seal may spend up to an
...r slowly eating in this way.

Giants of the seas

INUIT CARVING
This Inuit model of a sperm whale is from Alaska. European whalers were influenced by Inuit carving when they began to engrave the teeth and bones of whales.

Epidermis

Dermis

Blubber can be 10 in (25 cm) thick

Connective tissue

Fascia

Muscles

HOT FAT
Under a whale's skin there is an insulating layer of fatty blubber. A network of blood vessels runs through it. If the whale overheats, more blood is pumped up nearer to the cold water, which cools down the whale.

About 150 pairs of yellowish white baleen plates filter plankton

THE POLAR SEAS are home to a whole range of whales. The gray, humpback, fin, and blue whales are summer residents, making good use of a rich supply of plankton. When winter comes, and the krill disperse to graze beneath the pack ice, most of the whales migrate to warmer waters near the equator. The narwhal, beluga, and bowhead whales remain in the Arctic all year round, and minke whales withstand the Antarctic winter. Whales do not feed much during the winter, relying on body fat to sustain them. Whales began to disappear when people hunted them in order to sell their oil, baleen (whalebone), and meat. Now that commercial whaling has declined, many whale populations have recovered.

SEA UNICORN
The spiral tusk of the male narw (*Monodon monoceros*) is an elong tooth. Tusks were traded outs the Arctic before most people I seen narwhals; this may have to the legend of the unicorn.

Blowhole on top of head for breathing; nostrils are closed off under water

Barnacles often themselves to a whale's skin and hi ride around the oc

ONE LONG VACATION
Gray whales make the longest migration journeys of any whale. They winter off the coasts of California and Mexico, then swim to their Alaskan feeding grounds for the summer, a round trip of more than 12,000 miles (20,000 km). Gray whales feed only in the summer, living off stores of energy in their blubber for the rest of the year. The young are born in the warmer waters of their winter home.

BONEFINGER
Inside a whale's flipper are the same bones as in our own hands. Flippers are used for steering and braking; the tail provides swimming power.

Two, or sometimes four, grooves on the throat

The sperm whale (*Physeter catodon*) can easily dive down to about 1,150 ft (350 m) and stay under for 10 minutes or longer. The longest recorded dive is 90 minutes, and dives occasionally reach 10,000 ft (3,000 m).

CLEVER KILLERS

whales (*Orcas*) live in pods of individuals that hunt together. are the fastest mammals in the ble to reach 35 mph (56 km/h). even tip seals off ice floes and sea lions from beaches. Nothing e from them, not even a blue whale.

Row of 6–14 humps on back instead of dorsal fin

THE BIG ONE

The largest animal that has ever lived, the blue whale (*Balaenoptera musculus*) is longer than a Boeing 737 jet and weighs 25 times more than an African elephant. Blue whales are now rare, since they were brought close to extinction by commercial whaling.

Large, strong muscles in the tail power the flukes; about a third of a whale's body is pure muscle

Flat, rigid tail flukes, stiffened with cartilage, move up and down to push the whale through the water

Killer whale

Fish

Seal

Seabird

Minke whale

Squid

Krill

Plankton

URAL BALANCE

whales are the top vores in many sub-Arctic ub-Antarctic food chains, and vital part of the food webs of seas. Their prey includes fishes, penguins, and other whales. rmen are often in conflict with whales because they believe the es take valuable fish stocks. But hales are part of the natural ce of life in the oceans, easily t by people overfishing.

GIANT FILTERS

Some whales, such as the right whale, gray whale, humpback whale, and blue whale, filter food from the seawater with fringed brushes, called baleen, inside their mouths. These whales have huge, arched jaws from which the baleen plates hang like curtains. Like fingernails, baleen is made of a substance called keratin.

A herding life

PEOPLE HAVE SURVIVED in the inhospitable Arctic regions of northern Scandinavia and the northern regions of Russia and Siberia for thousands of years. Native Arctic peoples followed a nomadic (traveling) hunting and fishing lifestyle, adapting to the intense winter cold, darkness, and snow without the aid of modern technology. Starvation and death by exposure were constant threats. Native peoples of the Eurasian Arctic include the Saami, or Lapps, of northern Scandinavia, and the Yugyt, Chukchi, Evenks, and Nenets of Siberia and northeastern Asia. Some Chukchi families still follow wild reindeer herds, hunting or lassoing them for their meat and pelts. Reindeer provided Arctic peoples with all their basic needs – food, clothing, tents, tools, and items to trade. In some remote areas, the native peoples still follow a traditional hunting lifestyle. But many now work in villages or towns, and some combine the old and new ways of life.

Staff is made of iron

SPIRIT POWER
In many traditional Siberian societies, a specially trained *angakok*, or shaman, acted as the link between the supernatural and natural worlds. A shaman fulfilled many roles, from doctor and meteorologist to performer of miracles. This shaman's headdress is embroidered with reindeer hair.

Shaman's head ornament from the Ostyak-Nenet tribe of Siberia

HANDY IN WINTER
This ivory carving of reindeer pulling a sled comes from central Siberia. Many Siberian tribes used reindeer as pack and draft (pulling) animals for carrying their household goods. Today, some reindeer herders hire out their reindeer sleds for transportation during the winter.

Foot represents a bear's paw

Bag is of stre reindeer

IN A TRANCE
Shamans of the Tungus tribe, east of the Yenisey River in central Siberia, held this staff while meditating. The shaman often went into a trance and spoke with the voice of a spirit "helper."

PACK YOUR BAG
The northern Komi lived to the west of the Ural Mountains, in northeastern Europe. They filled this *patku*, or knapsack, with clothes and other smaller items, and loaded it onto a baggage sled when following reindeer herds.

diff parts (reina body pro the bag's decor

MOVING CAMP

Because nomadic people often moved several times a year, their tents had to be simple and lightweight as well as sturdy. The tents usually had a conical framework of wooden poles, covered with several reindeer skins. The top of the tent was left open to allow smoke from the fire to escape.

...t tent,
...ia

A great deal of heat is lost through the head, so a hood is vital for keeping the head and ears warm in freezing conditions

Seams are very finely stitched to make the garment as warm and waterproof as possible

...t child's
...d winter parka

HUNTER OR HUNTED?

This hooded jacket from the Aleutian islands, between Siberia and Alaska, is made from strips of seal or walrus intestine, sewn together to make a waterproof garment. By dressing in the skins or fur of the animals, the hunter was making an important point – he became part of the animal world around him by taking on the appearance of the hunted.

Reindeer gut was often used for sewing skins together

Mittens are sewn right into the sleeves for extra warmth and protection

Fur trim was decorative, but also protected against icy winds

ORIGINS OF THE PARKA

The traditional winter coat of the Nenet tribe of northern Siberia consisted of a thick, warm long-sleeved jacket called a parka. The coat was sewn together from pieces of reindeer skin. The reindeer hide was worn on the outside; for the inner clothing, softer fur was placed next to the skin for extra warmth. Woolen undergarments provided added protection, and helped to trap body heat. Some people still wear traditional clothes, but most buy winter clothes made of synthetic materials.

Hunters of the north

The model has a traditional hairstyle

Strips of white hide from underside of caribou are used as decoration

Inuit clothes were often heavily embroidered

Both men and women wore sealskin boots called kamiks

INUITS, CALLED ESKIMOS by 19th-century Europea are the original inhabitants of the Arctic tundra northern Canada, Alaska, and Greenland. Al 100,000 Inuits still live there. Inuits and rela peoples were nomadic hunter-gatherers. Th lived near the coast in summer, building u food reserves for the winter. The rest of th year they traveled, hunting caribou, seals polar bears, and whales, and using every part of the animals they caught for food, shelter, clothing, weapons, and tools. Inui society was organized in extended family groups, with each member carrying out a specific job according to sex, age, and stat Games, music, and storytelling helped to pass the long winter hours. Most modern Inuits live in permanent settlements, often combining a regular job with hunting trips.

WINTER WARMTH
This traditional man's winter costume is made of caribou skin. Women sewed the skins together with sinew and a bone needle, and sometimes decorated the clothes with beadwork or embroidery. Only the families of good hunters replaced their clothes each year. Poor families unable to get caribou skins in the fall wore their clothes for more than a year, or had to make their parkas out of sealskins.

Only the tiniest area is exposed to the freezing air

ANCIENT ART
Inuits carved elaborate animal figures out of walrus ivory, caribou antlers, and whale or seal bone. They used ivory bow drills as instruments. This Inuit carving of a woman standing on a seal comes from Baffin Island. Today, Inuit artists use modern tools and soapstone to make carvings for tourists.

Sealskin jacket protected hunter from icy Arctic winds

Hunter pulled on line attached to harpoon to haul seal out of the water

Fitte holds harpoo

A seal bladder float was attached to any large catch so that it would float behind the canoe art, such as this wooden mask, often [depic]ted the supernatural world and [ac]tivities of the shamans. Only a [sham]an would have worn a mask [like t]his, but the Inuit also made [a vari]ety of small bone and [s]tone maskettes for rituals [and c]eremonies. They also [made] carvings of abstract [shape]s, and of natural [subjec]ts such as animals.

Mask was held on by leather straps that ran through holes at the side

Slit for eye

Shaman's wooden mask, Barrow Point

Woodworms, which do not exist in Arctic temperatures, have pitted this mask since it was collected for a museum

[SHO]RT-LIVED SEAL
[Th]e Inuits copied polar bears in [their] hunting techniques, catching [seals] at their breathing holes in the [wint]er ice. Dogs were used to sniff [out t]he breathing hole if it had [beco]me covered by snow. When [the s]eal emerged, the hunter thrust [in hi]s harpoon, pulled out the seal, [and] dragged it to his sled.

Animal carvings were believed to give a hunter special powers

TOOL FOR THE JOB
This carved wooden club was used by the Haida tribe of Canada for killing seals. The Inuit believed in respecting the animals they hunted. A dead animal was beheaded to release its spirit, and sometimes a small part of a marine mammal was returned to the sea to encourage rebirth.

Boat is covered with sealskin

Light wooden paddle for rowing through ice

Sharply pointed harpoon

KAYAK
The Inuit used kayaks to hunt sea mammals such as seals and whales. Kayaks were one-man hunting craft, completely enclosed except for an opening for the hunter to climb in at the top. Umiaks were larger, open hide-covered boats used for transporting goods and people, and also for hunting whales.

Discovering the Arctic

Norwegian flag

IN THE 15TH CENTURY, European powers, intent on trade expansion, sponsored voyages into uncharted waters. Much early European exploration was centered on the search for a northern sea route to China and India, which would halve the time and danger involved in traveling overland. After the discovery of America, two routes were envisioned: the Northwest Passage, following the American coast, and the Northeast Passage, along the Siberian coast. The search for the Northwest Passage was soon monopolized by the British and the French but was later joined by the Americans; the Dutch and the Russians concentrated on the northeast. Over the next 350 years explorers opened up the Arctic, but it was not until 1878 that a Swede, Adolf Nordenskjïld, navigated the Northeast Passage, and 1905 when the great Norwegian explorer Roald Amundsen sailed through the Northwest Passage.

UP AND AWAY
Salomon Andrée, a Swedish aeronaut, and two companions tried to reach the North Pole in the balloon *Örnen* (*Eagle*) in 1897. The balloon was weighed down by ice and forced to land. All three men perished.

Sir John Franklin 1786–1847

Medal

Fox collar

RESCUE FOXES
Eight foxes were released in the Canadian Arctic wearing collars bearing the name and position of a rescue ship, and medals were distributed among the local people. It was hoped they might encounter Franklin survivors.

THE SEARCHERS
In 1845 Sir John Franklin led 128 men on a search for the Northwest Passage. By 1847 nothing had been heard from them, and his wife mobilized many expeditions to hunt for them. In fact, they had all died, but the searches greatly advanced geographical knowledge of the Arctic.

THE HOMECOMING
In 1818 John Ross (leading the procession), returned home to England, having failed to find the Northwest Passage but having succeeded in killing a bear! This cartoon was by George Cruickshank.

Small slits let in
minimum glare

Sails made of
strong canvas

SNOW BLINDNESS

The rays of the Arctic sun shining on snow
are dazzling. The light can cause temporary
blindness and may damage the eyes. Arctic
peoples fashioned goggles from leather or
occasionally wood. Early explorers followed
their example. These goggles belonged to Sir
William Parry, who had traveled far north in
search of the Northwest Passage and was later
one of the searchers for Sir John Franklin's
ill-fated expedition.

THE PASSAGE SAILED

In 1903, aboard an old fishing boat
called the *Gjoa*, loaded with three
years' provisions, the Norwegian
explorer Roald Amundsen and
six companions set out to
navigate the Northwest
Passage. On the way, they
spent two years on King William
Island studying the Inuit way of
life and collecting scientific data.
In 1905 the *Gjoa* set off again and
reached the Pacific. Fifty years
earlier, in 1850–54, Captain
Robert McClure and his crew had
made the journey east-to-west, doing
the central part of it on foot after
losing their ship, but Amundsen
was the first to sail through.

Chocolate was left in
Canada by Sir James Ross's
expedition in 1849

Two larger boats
were carried, as well
as the small lifeboat

Dried biscuit
was staple fare

Tripe de roche

Auxiliary engine
fitted to the ship

Small lifeboat

Barrels
containing
water

FOOD FAILURE

Many expeditions failed because the food
supplies taken were either inadequate or
insufficient in quantity. The value of
carbohydrates was not known, and many
explorers suffered from scurvy through
lack of vitamin C. Explorers tried to
utilize natural resources like *tripe de roche*,
a kind of lichen, on which Captain
Parry's sailors lived in 1824.

Scott and the Antarctic

Surveying the land

At the beginning of the 20th century, several nations wanted to explore the Antarctic. In 1910, Robert Scott (1868–1912) from Britain set out for the South Pole. His expedition also had scientific objectives. After first using motorised sleds, ponies and dogs, and then hauling their own sleds through the harsh terrain, Scott and four companions, Wilson, Bowers, Oates, and Evans, finally arrived at the pole only to find that Norwegian explorer Roald Amundsen had reached it weeks before them. On the return journey the weather worsened, and weakened by cold and hunger, all five men perished. But although they lost the polar race, their scientific studies greatly advanced Antarctic science.

RUNNING REPAIRS
Dr. Wilson took this sewing kit on the ill-fated 1910–12 expedition. Keeping cotton and canvas clothing in good repair was essential in the harsh and difficult conditions.

Microscope magnifies the image inside the instrument

Compact and lightweight kit for traveling

Side mirror reflects light into the instrument

Günther & Tegetmeyer
BRAUNSCHWEIG, No 4716

NICKEL
TRADE MARK
SAFETY + PIN
WARRANTED

BASE CAMP
From this desk in his "den" in base camp at Cape Evans, Scott wrote letters, reports, and his diary, studied maps, and planned the details of his trek to the pole. The extreme cold and the dry atmosphere have preserved the hut virtually as it was in 1910.

ELECTRIC SPIDER
This electrometer, taken by Scott to Antarctica, was used to measure tiny fluctuations in atmospheric electricity. If there was a difference in electric charge between the earth and the atmosphere, a small suspended mirror inside the electrometer would move. This movement was compared against the fixed line of a suspended fine filament from a black widow spider's web.

Wire to ground the instrument

SUN ROUTE

This compass was used on Scott's 1910 expedition. From the time on a watch and the known position of the sun in the sky at that time, explorers could figure out a north-south direction using the compass and a chronometer.

*ng attached
pass to a
ly point*

POCKET HOSPITAL

A tiny medical kit was an essential part of polar expeditions. Injuries and frostbite had to be treated quickly in the harsh conditions.

Tablets of painkillers such as morphine and cocaine

Poisons such as strychnine were used for medicinal purposes

Syringe for administering standard doses of medicine

NEW LIFE

The *Terra Nova*, the ship in which Scott sailed to Antarctica on his last expedition, was originally a Scottish whaling vessel. Scott sailed to Cape Evans on Ross Island and set up his base camp there.

Instrument made mostly of brass so not affected by magnetic fields

LAST BASE

This pile of rocks marks the spot where the bodies of Scott, Wilson, and Bowers are buried. Only 11 miles (18 km) from a food depot, they were exhausted from hauling supplies and over 35 lb (15 kg) of geological specimens.

rst to the pole

Norwegian explorer Roald Amundsen
72–1928) chose a different route to the
e than Scott. He also started his journey
ser to the pole than Scott, setting up
e camp at Framheim on the Ross Ice
lf. Amundsen's expedition was better
pared and organized for fast travel
n Scott's. They also took along more
d. His polar party consisted of expert
ers and navigators and relied heavily
their dogs for transportation, and
r, as food.

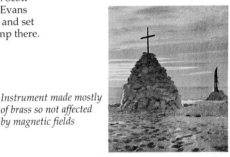

ANTARCTICA

South Pole

Transantarctic Mountains

Amundsen's route

Scott's route

Ross Ice Shelf

Scott's last camp
Cape Evans

Framheim

Ross Sea

FLYING THE FLAG

Amundsen set out for the South Pole on October 20, 1911, across the previously explored Axel Heiberg glacier. He reached pole on December 14, beating Scott by just ver a month. Amundsen also made several editions to the Arctic, flying over the North in the airship *Norge* in 1926. He was lost in a rescue mission in the Arctic in 1928.

Keeping warm and safe

EARLY EXPLORERS SUFFERED greatly because they did not know how to keep warm and, equally important, dry, in harsh conditions. The freezing power of the icy winds was also largely ignored. Frostbite was very common and many men died of exposure. In time, lessons were learned from the native peoples, and by the early years of this century, equipment had improved enormously. Explorers used sleeping bags and fur boots and wore canvas jackets to protect themselves from the icy winds. Bringing the right food supplies was extremely important. On many early expeditions, too much emphasis was placed on the need for meat, and carbohydrates, vital for energy, were largely ignored. Today a great deal is known about the foods necessary for a healthy diet.

FIGURE OF FUR
Amundsen's clothing was typical of that worn in the early 1900s.

LAYER BY LAYER
The inadequacy of the clothes they wore contributed to the deaths of Captain Scott and his companions. They sweated a lot; the sweat froze, making the body cold and the clothes heavy and uncomfortable. Layers of lightweight clothes would have allowed good ventilation with the trapped air insulating against the cold.

Polypropylene fabric takes moisture away from the body, preventing heat loss caused by sweat evaporation

Inner layer: "long johns" worn next to the skin

Potato

Bolognaise sauce   Shepherd's pie

Cooking vessel

Removable inner sole

TRAVELING LIGHT
Traveling in the freezing polar landscapes is hard work, whether on skis or by snowmobile or sled. Therefore, food has to be light and compact and quick and easy to prepare. Dried foods that only have to be mixed with heated ice or snow fulfill all the requirements and are also nutritious.

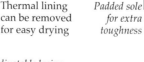

Thermal lining can be removed for easy drying

Padded sole for extra toughness

FEET FIRST
The feet and the hands are particularly vulnerable to frostbite, so it is essential that these parts of the body are adequately covered. Today, different types of footwear have been designed for different conditions.

Adjustable lacing ensures a good fit

Glacier boots for use in deep powder snow

Thick, ridged rubber soles help prevent slipping

EYE SHADES
Goggles are worn to protect eyes from windblown snow and the glare of sunlight reflected off snow and ice.

Middle layer: fiberpile undergarment traps a layer of air, which is warmed by the body

ICE CRACKER
When climbing steep ice, two ice axes are hammered into the ice face. The climber then uses them to pull himself up.

Zippers allow garments to be easily removed

...proof nylon ...ing keeps the ...down from ...ing wet and ...insulating ...ncy

Outer layer: jacket

Adjustable wrists prevent snow from entering mitt

For delicate outside work, thermal inner mitts are worn alone

Waterproof outer mitts are lined with fiberpile fabric for warmth

POLAR MAN
One of the many advantages of layer dressing is that the number of layers can be adjusted according to the activity of the wearer and the temperature. This outer layer, consisting of jacket and trousers, is filled with pure high-quality goosedown, which is the most efficient of natural fillings. Combined with the mid- and base layers, these garments provide insulation sufficient to keep warm at -40° F (-40° C).

Outer layer: high, padded trousers

Crampons attached to the soles provide grip

FOOT SUPPORT
These climbing boots are made of strong and fairly stiff plastic that supports the foot and ankle. They have a removable thermal lining.

...nal ...worn to ...kin

Padded socks add extra warmth and help keep the feet dry

Polar travel

THE FIRST SNOWMOBILE
Scott's motorized sled was the first vehicle with caterpillar tracks to be designed especially for snow. The slats on the tracks helped to grip the snow. The vehicle was far ahead of its time, but it had an unreliable early gasoline engine and soon developed serious mechanical faults in the severe Antarctic environment. But it was a forerunner of the snowmobiles of today.

THE SNOW AND ICE of polar regions have always posed special problems for travelers. Snowshoes and skis keep people from sinking too far into soft snow, and boots with rough or spiked soles grip icy ground. Long, low sleds on smooth runners red friction and make it easier to move heavy loads over slippery, frozen surfaces. Early polar explorers learned from native Ar peoples the benefits of using husky dogs to pull sleds. (Noma Lapp people used reindeer for the same purpose.) Modern motorized vehicles, such as the snowcat, with clawlike grips, the snowmobile, with skis underneath, were developed from tried and tested traditional forms of transportation.

POLAR HORSESHOE
The pressure of a horse's or pony's hooves drives straight down through the snow, causing them to sink up to their bellies. The hooves also break through sea ice and snow bridges very easily. Snowshoes for horses and ponies help to spread out the weight so they have more chance of staying on the surface.

"Tennis racket" shape to spread weight as evenly as possible

A BRAVE MAN'S SHOES
These snowshoes were worn by Captain Oates, who perished on Scott's 1910–12 expedition to Antarctica. Oates's feet became frostbitten on the return journey, and then gangrenous. Rather than hold his companions up, he walked out of Scott's tent in a blizzard to die, so that they would be free to press on as fast as possible. His last words were "I am just going outside and may be some time." He hoped that this would enable his companions to save themselves, but tragically, his heroic gesture did not have the result he desired.

TOBOGGAN RUN
Sleds used in the Arctic and Antarctic need to be strong enough to carry heavy loads, but light enough for dogs or people to pull. Different types of sled suit different conditions. Narrow runners are best for hard ice, wide runners for soft snow. This wooden sled dates from 1934–37 and is loaded with scientific equipment, food, and medical supplies. A team of 12 huskies can pull a fully loaded sled weighing half a ton.

Shovel for digging snow

Wooden runners have iron on top to make them stronger and sturdier

Flat-bottomed sled like a toboggan "floats" easily over the surface of the snow without sinking in too far

24   66   1 5

CANOEING THE SNOW

Traditional methods of travel in Lapland included various types of canoe-shaped sleds called *pulkkas*. These had one runner only and were usually pulled by reindeer. A common kind of *pulkka* was large enough for one adult passenger, who sat with his legs outstretched, ready for braking. A wider *pulkka* was used to transport belongings. A third kind of *pulkka* was used by the Skolt Lapps for carrying sick people, children, and belongings. Reindeer were harnessed three abreast to this *pulkka*.

E SIGHT

Lapp people
as nomads,
ting from
to place,
used reindeer
k animals, or
sleds. Today
arely do so,
se most Lapp
es have settled in
es, although they
eep reindeer.

OTH MOVERS

e heavy wooden skis were used by Scott
s first expedition to Antarctica in 1901–04.
can be used on most kinds of snow and ice.
spread out the weight of a person, helping
to stay on the surface of the snow. They
reduce friction, sliding easily over snow
ce and allowing greater distances to be
red than by walking.

wooden cases loaded with
tific equipment, food, and
medical supplies

Canvas cover for
protecting supplies

SNOW DOGS

The husky dogs used to pull sleds are social animals, working in a strict hierarchy under their leader in the sled team. They are hardy, strong, and intelligent, but compulsive fighters. Huskies can survive freezing temperatures curled up in snowdrifts. The snow acts as an insulating blanket, helping to keep them warm at night or during blizzards.

"WITH CAPTAIN SCOTT AT THE SOUTH POLE"
Fry's **Cocoa**
PURE
& CHOCOLATE

MAKERS TO
H.M. THE KING.

DRIVEN TO THE DOGS

Sleds pulled by dogs are one of the best means of moving heavy loads over ice and snow. Usually, it takes at least a year or two of hard practice to learn how to drive a dog sled.

Life at the poles

THE CRUEL SEAS, savage and unpredictable climates, and inhospitable terrains of the two polar regions have ensured th[at] neither environment has ever been completely conquered b[y] humans. The history of polar exploration is one of appallin[g] hardship and terrible toll of human life. However, in the Arctic, the Inuit peoples evolved survival skills over the centuries that enabled them to live a fruitful existence. European explorers learned much from their way of life and gradually applied this knowledge to their own ability to explore and live in these harsh environments. Today, the lifestyle at the poles for both Inuits and oth[er] polar dwellers is very similar. Scientific advan[ces] in clothing, transportation, food, and building have ensured a way of life far removed from th[e] hardships of earlier times.

HELPING HANDS
Many early explorers died because they could not build strong enough shelters. By the 19th century, Arctic explorers realized how much they could learn from the native peoples.

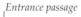

EFFICIENT RECYCLING
On Scott's last expedition, Edward Wilson made a successful candlestick out of a cracker box. Explorers tried to find an alternative use for everything.

Window made from a block of freshwater ice

Entrance passage   *Storage alcove*

OVERNIGHT STAY
Today, some Inuits still build igloos as temporary shelter. Here the hunter is lighting his primus stove, with which he will warm himself and cook his dinner.

SNOW HOUSE
Contrary to popular belief, Inuits never built igloos as permanent homes, but as temporary bases during the winter seal-hunting season. For much of the time they lived partly underground in dwellings made on a frame of driftwood or whalebone and covered by grass.

Gas shaft

Main access shaft

Office block housing specialized scientific areas

Garage

Library

Lounge

Dormitory block

Infirmary; most illnesses are treated on the station

...n

...ining room

Sled stores

MODERN CONVENIENCES

...y several countries have large research stations in the
...rctic, some permanent and some temporary. Most
...ns are involved in scientific surveys in geology,
...hysics, glaciology, terrestrial biology, and atmospheric
...ces. Several stations, like Britain's Halley Station, have
...built underground. Halley has been built four times,
...ch of the successive structures has been crushed by the
...ily shifting ice sheet.

SKIDDING AROUND
Polar travel is no
longer reliant on dogs
or ponies. Today most
people travel on
snowmobiles, which
are small motorized
sleds on skis. They are
easy to maneuver and
pull very heavy loads.

...bber
...amp

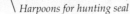

Women wear leather
inner garments

Wooden sleeping
platform covered
with furs

LAB OF THE NORTH
Canada has several
research laboratories
in the Arctic. This
space-age laboratory
at Igloolik in Canada's
Northwest Territories
has contributed much
to scientific knowledge
of the Arctic region.

Frame for drying skins

Harpoons for hunting seal

Domino-
shaped blocks
of frozen snow

Last frontiers

A<small>T</small> THE HEIGHT OF SUMMER in the Antarctic, tourist ships move gently around the coast. Even 30 years ago such sights would have been unthinkable, but today people are willing to pay large sums of money to see the last real wilderness in the world. In the Arctic, careless human exploitation in the past has damaged the fragile ecosystem. Today concerned governments are trying to find ways to develop the region while caring for the very special natural environment. Because the Antarctic is less accessible than the Arctic, it is still largely undamaged by humans, although holes in the ozone layer above the Antarctic have already been discovered. Many people believe that one way to preserve the area is to make the whole region into a world park, with every form of exploitation internationally banned. It is important to conserve the Arctic and Antarctic so that future generations can experience these extraordinary environments with their unique wildlife in their natural state.

DAY TRIPPERS
Tourist visits to the Antarctic have to be carefully monitored a[nd] organized, as tourists damage fragile vegeta[tion] and disturb nesting ar[ea] breeding grounds. On [the] other hand, tourist vis[its] can help to spread con[cern] for conservation.

GARBAGE DISPOSAL
The way people dispose of their trash in the Arctic and Antarctic often pollutes or damages the environment. Garbage dumps on the edge of Churchill, Canada, attract polar bears, which can be poisoned or injured by eating the garbage. The bears' nearness also causes fears for people's safety.

All snowflakes have six points

LANDS OF SNOW
The permanence of snow and ice in the Arctic and Antarctic is what makes these regions unique. Snow reflects the sun's rays, helping to keep temperatures low at all times.

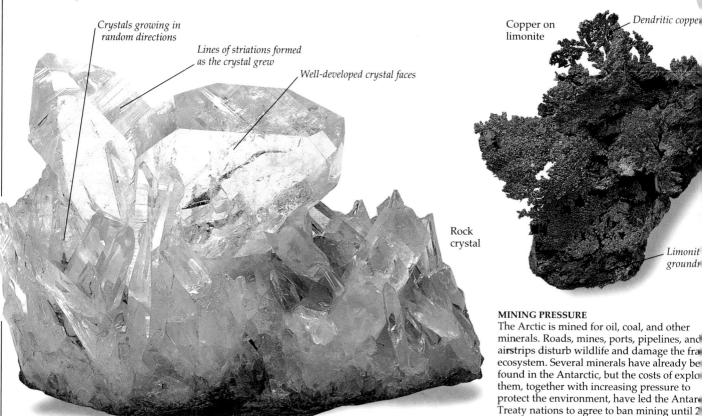

Crystals growing in random directions

Lines of striations formed as the crystal grew

Well-developed crystal faces

Copper on limonite

Dendritic coppe[r]

Rock crystal

Limonit[e] groundm[ass]

MINING PRESSURE
The Arctic is mined for oil, coal, and other minerals. Roads, mines, ports, pipelines, and airstrips disturb wildlife and damage the fra[gile] ecosystem. Several minerals have already be[en] found in the Antarctic, but the costs of explo[iting] them, together with increasing pressure to protect the environment, have led the Antar[ctic] Treaty nations to agree to ban mining until 2[041].

Purpose area represents
area of lowest ozone

Orange and white
areas show regions
of highest ozone

Krill are omnivores – they
eat other crustacea, krill,
and phytoplankton

Krill filter phytoplankton and
other food from the water with
their feathery feeding apparatus

ES OVER THE POLES
t 15 miles (25 km) above the
, a layer of gas called ozone
ds the Earth from the sun's
iolet rays. Holes in this layer
first discovered over the
rctic, but they also occur over
rctic, because of the special
her conditions in the polar
ns. Gases called CFCs are
ably to blame. They are
mainly in aerosols,
erators, and
nditioning.

At night, the luminescent
organs of krill shimmer
in the darkness

Bulbous eyes

Female krill spawn twice a year, laying
2,000–3,000 eggs, which sink into deep water

Krill are just 2 in (5 cm) long
but sometimes occur in such
vast numbers that they turn
the ocean red

POLAR RESEARCH
Many countries do research into the
wildlife, geology, and climate of the
Antarctic. In 1961 an Antarctic Treaty was
signed, agreeing that all scientific research
should be peaceful and not harm the wildlife.
So far 40 countries have signed it. In the Arctic
the land is controlled by the
various Arctic nations.

FUNDAMENTAL FOOD
A shrimplike crustacean (shellfish)
called krill is the basis of most Antarctic
food chains, forming a vital food source
for whales and seals, and penguins and
other seabirds. A blue whale needs over
0.9 tons (900 kg) of krill to feel full! Krill
can live for six to seven years. In the
winter, they graze on phytoplankton (tiny
floating plants) under the ice. The reduction in whale
numbers caused by human hunting in the past caused krill
numbers to rise. Other krill-eating species, such as penguins
and fur seals, increased in numbers to exploit the extra food
source, upsetting the balance of existing food webs. The
long-term repercussions are as yet unknown. Krill may be
threatened by the holes in the ozone layer. The ultraviolet
light which penetrates through the holes can stop
phytoplankton from growing, so the krill have less to eat.

Index

Acknowledgments

Dorling Kindersley would like to thank:
Open Air Cambridge Ltd. for the use of their clothing and equipment; the staff of Tierpark Dählhölzli, Bern, Switzerland, for their time and trouble; Tony Hall at the Royal Botanical Gardens, Kew; Julia Nicholson and the Pitt Rivers Museum, Oxford; Robert Headland and the staff of the Scott Polar Institute, Cambridge; Whipsnade Zoo, Bedfordshire; The British School of Falconry, Gleneagles, Scotland; Ivan Finnegan, Kati Poynor, Robin Hunter, Manisha Patel, Andrew Nash, Susan St.Louis, and Aude van Ryn for design and illustration assistance.
Additional photography: Lynton Gardiner at the American Museum of Natural History (60/61b); Neil Fletcher (1c); Dave King (37cr); Minden Pictures

(42cl); Harry Taylor at the Natural History Museum (45tl, 47tr); University Museum, Cambridge (43cr); Jerry Young (16cl, 17c, 32/33, 40tl)
Index:
Hilary Bird
Maps:
Sallie Alane Reason
Model:
Gordon Models

Picture credits
t=top b=bottom c=centre l=left r=right

Aardman Animations: 28cr
Ardea: 36c; /Jean-Paul Ferrero 28bc; /François Gohier 45cr; /Graham Robertson 30c
B & C Alexander: 6/7b, 8bl, 11ctr, 15t, 21c, 23c, 25br, 38tl, 39tcr, 42bl, 42/43b, 44bl, 44br, 59c, 60cbl, 61cbr, 62tl, 62tr; /Paul Drummond 23tl; /NASA 63tl
Barnaby's Picture Library /Rothman: 6/7c

Bridgeman Art Library: 25tl; /British Library 7tl; /National Maritime Museum 52cl
British Antarctic Survey: 10tr, 12ctl, 23bl; /D.G. Allan 13 tr, 13br; /C.J. Gilbert 10cl, 10bl, 12tl; /E. Jarvis 45br ; /B. Thomas 61cr
Bruce Coleman Ltd: 14/15b, 34tl, 35bl, 36bl, 36br; Jen & Des Bartlett 20cl /Roger A. Goggan 12/13; /Johnny Johnson 7tr; /Stephen J. Krasemann 19br; /Len Rue Jr. 40bl; /John Shaw 41c; /Keith Nels Swenson 11ctl; /Rinie van Meurs 29cr
ET Archive: 6tr
Mary Evans Picture Library: 8tl, 9tr, 38tr, 40cr, 41tr, 42tl, 46tr, 54bl, 55ct, 55cr, 55bc, 56tl
Illustrated London News: 20tl, 26cr
Frank Lane Picture Agency: /Hannu Hautala 17tcl; /E&D Hosking 22c; /Peter Moore 14cl; /F. Pölking 32cl; /Mark Newman 38c; /Tony Wharton 17tl
Natural History Photographic Agency: /B&C Alexander 10/11; /Melvin Grey 20/21b; /Brian Hawkes 29tl; /Tony Howard / ANT 10c; /E.A. James 29tr;

/Peter Johnson 27c; /Stephen Krasemann 37tr; /Lady Philippa Scott 27bl
Robert Opie Collection: 59cr
Oxford Scientific Films: 27ctl; /Doug Allan 12c, 12b, 16bl, 30tl, 44ctr; /Michael Brooke 22tl; /S.R. Maglione 14/15t; /Colin Monteath 22b; /S.R. Morris 35cl; /Owen Newman 20ctl; /Ben Osborne 26bl, 28l, 29b; /Richard Packwood 36tl; /Konrad Wothe 32bcr
Planet Earth Pictures: /Gary Bell 33tcl; /Peter Scoones 29tc; /Scott McKinley 9cr; /Bora Merdsoy 13bl
Royal Geographical Society: 53cr, 53tr, 56cl; /Alastair Laidlaw 53br
Science Photo Library: /Dr. David Millar 63bl; /Claude Nuridsany & Marie Perennou 62cl
Zefa Picture Library: /Allstock 31c; /Frans Lanting 26tl

Every effort has been made to trace the copyright holders. Dorling Kindersley apologises for any unintentional omissions and would be pleased, in such cases, to add an acknowledgment in future editions.